The Boy from Sula

Lavinia Derwent is the author of the well-known 'Tammy
Troot' stories and many others. Her other Sula books, called
Sula and *Return to Sula* are also published in Piccolo.
She lives in Scotland.

Also by Lavinia Derwent in Piccolo

Sula
Return to Sula

Lavinia Derwent

The Boy from Sula

cover illustration by Prudence Seward
text illustrations by Felicity Lowe

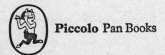
Piccolo Pan Books

First published in Great Britain 1973 by
Victor Gollancz Ltd
This edition published 1977 by Pan Books Ltd,
Cavaye Place, London SW10 9PG
© Lavinia Derwent 1973
ISBN 0 330 24888 X
Printed in Great Britain by
Richard Clay (The Chaucer Press), Ltd, Bungay, Suffolk

Contents

1 Far Away from Sula

The boy and the seal had been staring at each other for a long time without moving a muscle. Both looked lost and lonely, far from their familiar surroundings. What were they doing here, prisoned within walls in the great city of Glasgow?

The seal was in a glass case, dead and stuffed. The boy was alive, though almost as immobile.

At first Magnus had thought, with a sudden leap at his heart, 'It's Old Whiskers!'

He broke away from the group of boys being shown round the Museum, as alike as peas in a pod. Neat shorts, navy-blue blazers, school badges. Cronan High School. Magnus was dressed the same, but he hated it. It was a sign that he had been trapped like the seal and labelled

7

'schoolboy'. He would sooner have been scrambling over the rocks in Sula, wearing his old breeks and tattered jersey. Magnus Macduff, a free human being.

He took a closer look at the seal. It was not Old Whiskers. Of course not! He was alive, splashing in the sea around Sula. Or maybe sunning himself on a rock.

'I wish I was there,' thought Magnus with a sinking feeling of home-sickness. There was a bleak air about the Museum with its dead creatures and inanimate objects. He longed to look at something living and moving.

There were stranger sights to be seen than the stuffed seal. Bears and bison and elks. Prehistoric birds and beasts. Giant bats with peculiar names like *pternandon*, and a clumsy creature called a *tyrannosaurus*.

The schoolboys were gaping and giggling at the exhibits.

'Look at yon muckle big beast! What a monster! Isn't it a blessing he's dead?'

Magnus preferred the seal, dead or alive. He had been staring at it for so long that he began to imagine it was moving and breathing. The very sight of it seemed to bring Sula nearer, till he could almost smell the salty sea-air and see Gran stooping to pick up a load of peat. He could always see Gran when he was far away from her. At home he hardly ever looked at her. She was just there, like the aspidistra in its brass pot or the old tin bath lying in Cowan's field.

'Magnus Macduff!'

The teacher in charge was calling the boys to heel with a note of exasperation in his voice.

Mr John Craigie was a crumpled-looking man, as if he had been thrown together in a hurry. His suit needed pressing, his collar was adrift, his hair tousled, his shoelaces loose; even his nose was crooked, but his heart was in the right place. Usually he was easy-going and good-natured, but today he was worried and irritable.

It was no easy matter bringing twenty-five stirring schoolboys all the way from Cronan to Glasgow in a hired bus, and conducting them round a Museum and Art Gallery that held so many distractions. One by one they strayed into forbidden corners. It would have taken a sheepdog, like Rory, to round them all up.

Even during the bus-journey they were a restless lot, changing from seat to seat and thumping each other playfully with their fists. They ate crisps, chewed gum, used their school-caps as footballs, and exercised their lungs by shouting out tuneless ditties. *She'll be coming round the mountain* was their favourite.

Singing Ay Ay Yippy Yippy Ay. It was enough to give anyone a headache.

Mr Craigie sat at the back of the bus puffing gloomily at his pipe and wondering if it was worth while being an Art Master. Was he wasting his time trying to teach these young hooligans to appreciate the world's finest paintings? What did they care about Rembrandt or Van Gogh? They scarcely listened to what he told them. Art was merely another lesson to be endured. They would sooner be out in the playground punching each others' noses.

All except the boy from Sula. John Craigie brightened up when he saw Magnus sitting silently in front of him in the bus, fending off the blows of his classmates. Magnus could fight as well as any if he was in the mood. But if he wanted to be alone he could withdraw into his shell and no one knew how to winkle him out.

Magnus was the one pupil in the class who showed

9

any signs of promise. There was already the mark of natural genius in his drawings. With a few deft strokes the boy from Sula could fashion perfect pictures of seals, sea-birds, and all the wild creatures he had seen on his remote island. Magnus had the gift of bringing them to life, so that the sea-mews seemed to be streaking across the sky, the leverets leaping into the air, and the seals turning somersaults in the water. The boy must have studied every beak, claw, eye, feather, and whisker to draw them in such faithful detail.

For years John Craigie had longed to get his hands on such a pupil. It was worth the dull slog with the rest of the class to find one with the spark of genius inside him, and to feel that he was helping to fan it into flame.

'You'll be a famous name some day, Magnus,' he prophesied proudly.

'Away!' said Magnus, turning red in the face.

What did fame mean to the boy from Sula? All he wanted was to finish his term at the High School and get back to the island as soon as possible. He would stay there for ever, painting the seals and the sea-birds, and helping Gran on the croft. Beyond that, he had no ambition.

It had been difficult enough to lure him to the High School in the first place. Indeed, it had been a miracle that he had come to Cronan at all; and it was the eccentric little Duke from Cronan Castle who had acted as magician.

On a visit to Sula he and Magnus had become firm friends. Strange that a noble lord of ancient lineage and a boy as wild and untamed as Magnus should forge such a friendship. Yet in many ways the two were alike, each hiding his talents from other eyes. The Duke in his crumbling castle made music secretly, as Magnus drew pictures. Each lived in a withdrawn world of his own.

'Come and stay with me, boy,' he pleaded. 'Try it for one term. Who knows? With you there to inspire me, I might do something with my music at last. And a few painting-lessons won't do you any harm. It may be the making of us both. I promise you won't be hemmed in. There's plenty of space and lots of animals around the place. There's a Shetland pony called Sheltie ...'

It was not the thought of Sheltie and the other animals that swayed Magnus in the end. It was out of compassion for the lonely man that he made his great sacrifice. Leaving Sula for even a day would be a wrench. How could he survive a whole term on the mainland? Yet the pleading look in the Duke's eyes touched the boy's heart. It was like the look of a lost dog.

'I'll come,' he said gruffly. 'For a wee while.'

His decision had transformed the Duke's life, and made John Craigie feel that his daily grind as Art Master was worth while. Not that the boy from Sula was an easy pupil to teach. Half the time it seemed that Magnus was not in the classroom at all. It was only now and again that he came to life and began to sketch idly in his drawing-book, filling pages with pictures of crabs and crows, herons and hedgehogs, and a recurring picture of an old whiskered seal.

It was mainly because of Magnus that John Craigie had brought the class to Glasgow.

'Come along, boys,' he called out to them. 'It's time to look at the paintings.'

Magnus turned away from the seal, and the spell of Sula was broken. Mr Craigie was right. It was the paintings they had come to see. Famous pictures hanging on the Art Gallery walls. Mr Craigie had talked about them for hours in the stuffy classroom at Cronan, and shown them coloured pictures. Now they were to see the real thing.

Famous names went whirling through the boy's head. Dali. Picasso. Goya. Titian. Holbein. Michael Angelo ...

'Magnus Macduff!'

Startled, Magnus looked up when he heard the teacher call his name, as if he had seen a vision. Would his own name join the others one day? Perhaps schoolboys of a future generation would come and gaze at a *Magnus Macduff* in the Art Gallery.

The thought flared up and then flickered out. It was painting pictures that mattered, not being famous. Magnus took a last look at the stuffed seal, and followed the straggling schoolboys into the Art Gallery.

From then on time stood still for the boy from Sula. He was in a new world, full of wonder. He could have stared for ever at the works of Old Masters and of modern painters. A great longing came over him to find out their secrets and to strive to achieve such perfection. What a lot he had to learn! A lifetime would not be long enough.

'Take a look at this picture, boys.'

Mr Craigie was doing his best to explain about the paintings, but he was wasting his breath on such an inattentive audience. The schoolboys would sooner have been looking at the model ships and trains, or at the old weapons and armour. They were fed up with Art; they had enough of it at the High School. All except Magnus Macduff who was seeing visions that entranced him

When the others moved on, one of the boys came running back. He was a gentle creature, under-sized and nervous, the target for bullies. Wee Willy, they called him in class. He was the nearest Magnus had to a friend in the High School.

'Are you not coming, Magnus?' he asked in an anxious whisper.

'Uh-huh!' said Magnus automatically, but he did not move. He was miles away – centuries away – with the old painters.

Wee Willy tried again, clutching Magnus by the arm.

'Magnus, come on! The others are away.'

'I'm coming,' said Magnus. 'In a minute.'

It was a long minute. Wee Willy waited, shuffling his feet. Then he gave a sigh and trailed away after the rest. It was difficult enough to get through to Magnus at the best of times, but today the boy from Sula seemed to have gone beyond recall. It was best to leave him to himself and join the others gaping at the steam-engines.

*

A great silence had descended on the building. Magnus suddenly sensed it, though still feeling bemused after staring so long at the pictures. Now the people in the pictures seemed to be staring at him. Eyes followed him and heads turned to watch as he moved away to catch up with the rest of the class.

Not a whisper of sound could be heard. Where had they all gone? They were not looking at the prehistoric monsters, nor at the marble statues, the engines, or the armour. The seal in the glass case watched Magnus as he passed by. The creature seemed to be swaying from side to side as Old Whiskers did in the sea around Sula.

Magnus gave a shiver. It had grown dark and cold and eerie. There seemed no way out of the labyrinth of rooms, each leading to the other like a maze. All he could hear was his own breathing and the sound of his foot-steps.

At last he found his way to the great outer door and tried to open it, but it was firmly locked. Magnus rattled at the handle for a time, and then gave it up, realizing there was no means of getting out. He was locked in for the night amongst dinosaurs, pterodactyls' skeletons, and Egyptian mummies.

All around him the shadows grew more grotesque. The stuffed giraffes seemed to be stretching out their long necks. The wolf raised his head as if to howl. The prehistoric birds clenched their great claws ready to pounce. Armoured warriors loomed up brandishing their weapons.

Suddenly came the sound of clumping footsteps, as if one of the great beasts was on the prowl.

'Who's there?'

A booming voice echoed through the empty Museum. At first Magnus thought it was one of the warriors shout-ing at him. Then he heard the clanking of keys and felt himself grabbed by the scruff of the neck. It was a human hand that held him and a gruff human voice that asked angrily, 'What d'you think you're doing here?'

'Nothing,' said Magnus, trying to shake himself free.

He twisted round and found himself in the clutches of a nightwatchman with a red face and a moustache that was bristling with rage. The man had a look of Old Whiskers about him, only grumpier.

'Huh! A schoolboy!' he grunted, taking a closer look at Magnus. 'I might have known. Perfect nuisances! What have you got in your pockets, my lad?'

'Nothing,' said Magnus, trying to wriggle free; but the man held him in a tighter grip.

'Turn them out,' he said fiercely. 'At the double!'

Magnus reluctantly thrust his hands into his pockets. What did the watchman expect him to produce? A stolen Van Gogh, or a brontosaurus? There was little enough to show; only a stub of pencil, an elastic band, a safety-pin, and the old whistle he had made himself, the one he played in Sula when he wanted to attract the seals.

'What's this?' The man grabbed it and examined it closely.

'It's just a whistle.' Magnus reached out to take it back. It was one of his few treasured links with home. 'It's mine.'

'Hold on,' said the watchman, fending him off. He handed back the other items but kept a grip on the whistle. 'I might try a tune on it myself.'

Suddenly his moustache looked less bristly, and he had a kindlier note in his voice as he said, 'Come along, my lad. Let's have a cup of tea. This way.'

Magnus followed at his heels, not wanting to let the whistle out of his sight. The watchman clanked his keys as he led the way through one empty gallery after another till he reached a small cubby-hole where he had evidently made a refuge for himself.

On an old trestle-table lay a clutter of objects: a thermos flask, a transistor radio, the evening paper, a pair of spectacles, a pipe, and a cracked mug into which he poured some tea from the flask.

'Here, drink that, my lad,' he said, handing the mug to Magnus. 'I'll have a wee shot at the whistle.'

Magnus took a gulp of the strong sweet brew while the man pushed aside his moustache and blew out a few shaky strains of a tune that faintly resembled *I Belong to Glasgow*. He was no great musician, except in his own estimation. 'Not bad,' he said proudly. 'Would you like to hear *Annie Laurie*?'

Magnus was forced to hear it whether he liked it or not. He also had to listen to *John Brown's Body*, *Pop Goes The Weasel*, and *Happy Birthday To You* before the recital was mercifully interrupted by a shrill ring on the telephone.

'Blast!' said the watchman, laying down the whistle. His moustache began to bristle once more as he shouted into the receiver: 'Hullo! Who's there? Speak up!' He gave a sidelong glance at Magnus who had retrieved the whistle and was putting it back into his pocket. 'What? Yes, he's here. Locked in! Perfect nuisance! You'd better come and fetch him.'

He slammed down the receiver and grunted, 'School-boys! Pests! Come on, my lad; get moving. I'll have to go and open the door. They're coming to fetch you.'

Magnus was following him through the ghostly galleries when he caught sight of something gleaming in one of the glass cases. It was a chunk of stone, shooting off rays of colour: amber, pale pink, deep purple, almost like the Merry Dancers in the night sky over Sula. Indeed, everything about it reminded him of home. Suddenly he knew why.

'Where did that stone come from?' he asked the watchman eagerly.

'What?' The man turned round and peered at the glass case. 'Och! some wee island,' he said impatiently. 'Come on; get a move on.'

'What island?' persisted Magnus, tugging at his coat.

'How should I know?' said the man crossly. 'You can see for yourself, if you read the ticket.'

Magnus stared at the ticket in the dim light and read

the printed words. SULA STONE. Of course! Collected on the island by Mr Skinnymalink, the Hermit, and polished by him to bring out the hidden colours. No wonder it had reminded him of home!

'Well, are you satisfied now?' asked the watchman in a grumpy voice.

'Yes,' said Magnus, 'I'm satisfied.'

He felt a warm glow in his heart, knowing there was something from Sula in the great gloomy Museum, and an even warmer glow when he remembered that the school term was nearly over. Before long he would be back home.

*

In Sula the seals were barking and howling like dogs, a sure sign that a storm was coming from the west.

Sometimes they changed their tune to a plaintive wail, as if calling for help. The angry sea had begun to swirl, and the waves were tossing them like corks off their course.

Old Whiskers was leading, as befitted his age and wisdom. 'Follow me,' he grunted to the young seals as he battled his way through the restless water to find quieter quarters round the bay.

The young ones had enough sense to keep close behind him. Old Whiskers was often short-tempered, but they respected his judgement, knowing he could save them from a buffeting. The wind had already ruffled the washing-lines and was bending the rowan-tree in the Manse garden. It was best to stay close to the wise old one and obey his orders.

Old Whiskers raised his head and took a look at the little row of houses at the harbour. The waves were splashing over the rock where he and the boy used to meet. It had been a long time since they were together, lying on the rock in complete harmony. But the old seal sensed that Magnus had not deserted him for ever.

'Come along,' he called to the young ones. Then he plunged beneath the surface and bull-dozed his way to calmer waters.

Old Whiskers was not the only one in Sula who was thinking of Magnus. Young Jinty Cowan was trying to get in touch with him through the post-office telephone.

Living as she did in the Post Office and General Store, which was only one of the cottages at the harbour, she knew all about putting through calls. Jinty was bright; too bright sometimes. Full of wee plots and plans, most of them centred round herself. And Magnus.

She had a plot in her mind right now as she waited for her call to be put through. It was too stormy to go out and play, so what better could she do than talk to Magnus? To while away the time she sang a little tune.

'My bonnie lies over the ocean.'

Jinty had dressed up for the occasion, as if Magnus would be able to see her through the telephone, though he took little enough notice of her when they were face-to-face. She had put on her best jersey, the blue one with the Fair-Isle pattern, and tied her hair back with a choco-late-box ribbon. She was pleased with what she saw when she keeked in the little mirror advertising sheep-dip.

It was a pity, though, about the spots on her chin. Maybe she should ask the District Nurse for another bottle of tonic to clear them up. But she knew fine what Mrs Gillies would say.

'It's all that rubbish you eat, Jinty Cowan. You're always chewing away at something, like a sheep.'

True enough, Jinty had a liquorice-allsort in her

mouth right now. The trouble was she had a free hand to help herself from the boxes and bottles on the shop shelves. She was not tempted by the other goods on display: the tackety-boots, the binder-twine, the soap, and scrubbing-brushes. But it needed a stronger will than Jinty's to resist Turkish delight, macaroon bars, and whipped-cream walnuts when they were there for the taking.

Jinty swallowed the liquorice-allsort in one gulp when she heard a voice from the mainland saying, 'You're through.'

'Hullo,' said Jinty, loud and clear.

The woman who replied sounded old and shaky, but there was a Highland lilt in her voice. 'This is Cronan 1616.'

Cronan Castle! Now that the moment had come, Jinty's self-confidence began to dwindle. She took a startled look at herself in the mirror and blurted out, 'Could I speak to Mr M-Macduff?'

'Who?'

'Mr Macduff!' shouted Jinty into the receiver.

There was a pause before the old woman asked in a puzzled voice, 'Would it be Magnus Macduff you're wanting?'

'Yes, please,' said Jinty, breathing heavily. Who else? Her confidence was coming back, and she added in a firmer tone, 'Tell him it's Miss Cowan from Sula. Miss Jinty Cowan.' She exchanged glances with Miss Cowan in the mirror and gave herself a smug little nod.

'He's not in.'

'Not in!' The stuffing was temporarily knocked out of Miss Cowan. She had not bargained for this, and was not sure of her next move.

'He's away to Glasgow,' said the voice at the other end of the telephone. 'For the day.'

'Mercy me!' gasped Jinty.

Away to Glasgow! Magnus Macduff who never budged beyond Little Sula if he could help it.

Jinty was completely stumped. She breathed heavily into the receiver, and then heard the old woman saying, 'I'll see if His Grace is in.'

'His G-Grace!' said Jinty, beginning to tremble at the knees. It was one thing speaking to an ordinary mortal like Magnus, born and bred in Sula. It was a different matter making conversation with a Duke who lived in a castle and was related to the royal family.

Her face looked white in the mirror, except for the spots on her chin. Then suddenly her courage came back and she pulled herself up. After all, the Duke was just a wee man, as plain as porridge, in spite of his blue blood. 'Be bold, Jinty. Be bold,' she told herself.

'All right, I'll speak to the Duke,' she said in an assured voice. Then she added, half-hopefully, 'But maybe he's not in.'

2 Coming Home

The Duke was in all right, hiding in his favourite retreat, the Tower room at the top of the castle, where he kept his personal treasures and could play his fiddle in peace.

The room had a look of the Old Curiosity Shop about it. Everything lay higgledy-piggledy on the floor in untidy heaps, while a trio of dogs occupied the sagging sofa. Every available space was filled with old cricket-bats, tennis-racquets, model ships, butterfly-nets, riding-boots, stamp-albums, piles of tattered newspapers and music.

The story of a lifetime was here in the Tower room,

if it had been sorted out. But the Duke would not permit any tidying-up or sorting-out. He liked to rummage for himself till he found what he wanted. If it was dusty – well – he just blew the top layer off.

This was home to him, more than the vast lifeless rooms down below, filled with ancient furniture and family portraits. Up here he could shut himself away from the world and compose the music that kept singing through his head like a swarm of bees clamouring to be let out.

Since Magnus had come to live in Cronan Castle the Duke spent more and more time making music. The one seemed to inspire the other. While the boy painted the scenes of Sula, the Duke tried to capture the sounds of the island. Sheets of music were strewn on the floor, scrawled over with symbols conveying the cry of the gulls, the lapping of water against the rocks, the slither of a seal's body into the sea.

All his life the Duke had made up snatches of music, only to discard them. There had been no one to listen, or take an interest in what he was trying to do. But now it was different. With Magnus to listen and encourage him, he was determined that at last he would complete a whole symphony of musical sounds. The sounds of Sula.

He tried each phrase on his fiddle over and over again before putting it down on paper. Completely absorbed in his task, he was building up a complicated pattern of musical notes which an entire orchestra could play.

When Magnus was painting in the room next door, the singing of the violin-strings seemed to bring Sula nearer. It was almost like a duet, the one painting and the other playing in close harmony. But today the Duke could not find the right theme. He was missing the boy, even though he knew Magnus had only gone to Glasgow for the day.

He put aside the fiddle and wandered restlessly into the next room. The dogs scrambled down from the sofa and came scurrying after him. Magnus's room was tidier. The boy had fewer treasures to accumulate. The main feature was the easel set up by the window. Everything the Duke was trying to express in his music was there in the half-finished picture.

It was a familiar scene : the seal on the rock, the row of houses at the harbour with the Heathery Hill in the background, the *Hebridean* rounding Sula Point, and a figure bending to pick up a load of peat. Gran.

There were other pictures of the old woman propped up in a corner, showing the furrows in her face, the wrinkles round her eyes, the steel-grey hair drawn tightly back from her brow. She looked almost alive, as if she might turn round and call, 'Mag-nus! Bring in the cow. Mag-nus! Feed the hens. Mag-nus! Have you mended the net?'

The little Duke examined the pictures, then clapped his hands like a child. 'Well done, boy!' he cried out, pleased to see how the young artist's technique had improved. 'You've got it! It has been worth your while coming to Cronan.'

Certainly it had been worth it from the Duke's point of view. A breath of fresh air had entered into the castle, making the Duke feel younger and more alert. What would happen when Magnus went back to Sula? A sense of desolation came over the little man as he realised the term would soon be over, and Magnus would leave him to drift back into his old withdrawn ways.

'I'll go to Sula, too,' said the Duke, with a sudden

flash of inspiration. 'Yes, I will! Why not?'

He did a step-dance back into his own room, as excited as a schoolboy at the thought of scrambling up the Heathery Hill, fishing off Sula Point, playing long silent games of draughts with the Hermit, and continuing his companionship with Magnus. It was a splendid idea!

'Your Grace! Your Grace!'

'What?' called the Duke, still doing his step-dance.

'The telephone,' shouted old Bella, breathless after her climb to the landing below. 'You're wanted.'

'I'm not in.'

The Duke had a horror of the telephone and seldom bothered to answer it. Nasty noisy instrument. It was only silly chatterers who used it. Old Bella ought to have known better by now.

'It's somebody from Sula, Your Grace,' she called up to him. 'A Miss Jinty Cowan.'

Somebody from Sula! That was a different matter. The Duke descended the stairs with the dogs slithering after him. Jinty Cowan! He had a blurred picture of her, a nuisance of a child hovering at the Post Office door, waiting to waylay Magnus whenever he appeared. What on earth was *she* ringing up about?

He went down into the great hall hung with stags' heads, old shields and claymores, and picked up the receiver. He could hear a humming sound. Miss Jinty Cowan was singing to herself to keep her spirits up.

'*O bring back my bonnie to me.*'

'Hullo!' shouted the Duke.

The humming came to an abrupt stop. At the other end of the wire Jinty bobbed a quick curtsey in honour of the Duke and said in a breathless voice. 'H-Hullo, Your Grace. H-How are you?'

'What are you wanting?' roared the Duke, cutting out the small-talk.

'I was wondering,' began Jinty, and then stuck. Her face in the mirror looked so frightened that she almost dropped the receiver. Then she gave herself a little shake, took courage and blurted it all out in one sentence.

'I was wondering if I could maybe come across in the *Hebridean* to see Magnus and stay for a wee while till he comes back for the holidays, what do you think, Your Grace?'

'No!' said His Grace, loudly and firmly. He did not want a precocious child like Jinty running about the castle making a nuisance of herself. Nor was Magnus likely to welcome her presence.

'Oh well,' sighed Jinty, accepting defeat. It had been a good try, and she could always console herself with a whipped-cream walnut. But it would be a pity to leave it at that without making *some* contact with Magnus.

'Will you tell Magnus I was asking for him?' she appealed.

'M'm!' said the Duke, ready to lay down the receiver.

'Tell him that the twins are crawling,' said Jinty, anxious to pass on a piece of local news.

'What?' said the Duke, in a startled voice.

'Crawling,' repeated Jinty. 'The McCallum twins. Rose and Angus. They're growing quite big. The District Nurse says ...'

'Goodbye,' said the Duke firmly, and slammed down the receiver. A little of Miss Jinty Cowan went a long way. Through the open door he could see one of the peacocks preening its feathers on the overgrown lawn, and the old gardener scything away at the nettles. It was a pleasant enough scene, but today everything seemed dull without Magnus.

In the distance he caught sight of the *Hebridean* ploughing across the sea to Sula, and his fit of depression faded away.

'Soon we'll be on board, Magnus and I,' he thought, making his way up the great staircase with a lighter step. 'Summer in Sula! That's something to look forward to. By jove! so it is. But first, I've got to finish that music.' He took a running-jump up the last few stairs, leaving the dogs panting behind.

*

Next day Magnus heard the Duke calling to him from the Tower room next to his own.

'Listen to this, boy.'

Magnus had been staring out of the window, seeing pictures in the castle grounds. The deer rubbing their antlers against the trees, a crow sitting on a gatepost hunching his shoulders like an old man, the lordly peacocks striding across the lawn, a shaggy pony rolling over in the grass with its heels up in the air, the old gardener waging his never-ending battle with the nettles.

Inspired by his visit to the Art Gallery in Glasgow the boy had been roughing-out a new picture. He would have been content to keep on painting the scenes of Sula for ever, but Mr Craigie had urged him to break fresh ground.

'You can't go on repeating yourself, Magnus, like an echo. Try something new. There's more to be seen than Sula.'

Before he went to the High School Magnus had drawn and painted by instinct. He had not thought of right ways and wrong ways. But Mr Craigie had methods. The Art Master had to follow something called the curriculum. One lesson on still life, when they were all forced to draw an apple, a flower, or a jug. Another on faces, when one of the boys had to sit sideways on a stool while the others tried to draw his profile. It was all cut and dried.

As soon as he started being taught, Magnus became so inhibited that he could scarcely draw a line far less a Cox's orange pippin or Wee Willy's profile. Mr Craigie tried to explain to him all about perspective, about light and shade, about foregrounds and backgrounds; but Magnus seemed to be deaf. He sat as dumb as a dyke staring at his blank drawing-paper. Only when the teacher left him alone could he make his pencil or brush move in the old free manner.

Yet not quite the same. Though he seemed not to be listening, some of John Craigie's teaching was filtering through. Magnus found himself taking a more critical look at his work, and paying more attention to building up a balanced pattern. As time went by, he began to see what the teacher meant by his talk of perspective and all the rest. More so after his visit to Glasgow. Now he wanted to try even harder to find the right way.

The Duke called to him again in a louder voice. 'Magnus, come and listen to this.'

The boy had been vaguely aware of the ripples of music floating from the Duke's sanctum next door. It made a pleasant background to his work, as varied and colourful as the peacocks' feathers. Magnus sensed that there was something special about the music, and hoped it was not going to vanish into thin air as so many of the Duke's compositions did.

When he went through to the next room he found the

little Duke perched on a small stool, with sheet after sheet of manuscript strewn around him. His Grace was wearing an old toupee on his head. His thinking-cap.

He pushed it back from his forehead, twinkled his eyes at Magnus, and tucked his fiddle under his chin.

'I've finished it!' he said triumphantly. 'Listen, boy!'

The Duke played snatches of his composition while Magnus went and stood by the window, gazing out beyond the castle grounds to the sea. It was his favourite view, for Sula lay beyond the horizon; and now the Duke's music seemed to be bringing the island nearer. He had woven together all the familiar sounds till Magnus could almost see the sea-birds nesting on the cliffs and smell the peat-reek.

'Oh, Duke, that's great!' he cried out, when the little man paused and looked at Magnus to see what effect the music was having. 'It tells a story, about Sula.'

The Duke flushed with pleasure. 'That's it, boy! My new Sula Symphony. See!' He turned over the scattered sheets lying on the floor. 'It's all there. Not just for the violin. For a whole orchestra.'

'Well done, Duke!' A whole orchestra. 'Who's going to play it?' asked the boy. He knew nothing about orchestras, but he knew enough about the Duke to realize that he must urge him on. 'You're not to waste it,' he said fiercely. 'You'll have to do something with it.'

'You're right, boy. Wait! Let me think.'

He buried his face in his hands and sat silently on his stool for a moment, digging deep into the recesses of his mind. Magnus waited quietly till the little man sprang up.

'I've got it! I'll get in touch with Sir Ronald Some-body. Briggs! That's his name. Sir Ronald Briggs, the conductor fellow in London. Used to come and stay in the castle years ago. Years and years ago. He liked my music and was always urging me to go ahead with it. I'll write him a letter. I've got his address somewhere. Yes! that's what I'll do.'

He jumped from one foot to another with excitement, then shook Magnus warmly by the hand.

'It's all due to you, boy. I tell you what, if ever I get it published, I'll dedicate it to you. *To Magnus Macduff, without whom the Sula Symphony could never have been written.* And if it's performed in London, we'll go together to hear it.'

'London!' said Magnus. 'Mercy me!' It was more likely that he would go to the moon. But he would sooner be in Sula. Only a few more days and he would be back home.

*

When the great day came, Gran, who never showed her feelings except in practical ways, did a bigger baking than usual. Not just plain scones and oatcakes, but also a gingerbread, an apple-tart, and a batch of pancakes. *Dropscones*, Gran called them. They made a tempting display, set out to cool on a wire tray on the kitchen table.

From the cupboard she brought out a pot of home-made bramble-jelly as a treat, and gave a stir now and again at a pot of stovies bubbling by the fire. Upstairs Magnus's small room had been cleaned and tidied, and his old clothes laid out ready on the bed. It was Gran's way of saying something she could not express in words. 'Welcome home, laddie. I've missed you.'

Jinty Cowan was not so reticent. She had gone the whole hog. Dressed to kill in her best blue velvet frock, with a dab of scent behind her ears, she was clutching a tattered Scottish flag, complete with the lion rampant, ready to wave as soon as she saw the *Hebridean* rounding Sula Point. She had wanted to put up a WELCOME HOME banner above Gran's door, but the old woman had given her a look and said, 'Don't be daft, Jinty Cowan.'

Poor Jinty! Her life was full of rebuffs; but at least she could always bounce back like a rubber ball. As time dragged on and there was still no sign of the boat, she decided to go up to the Heathery Hill where she could catch her first glimpse of the boat even before it rounded the point. Magnus might be watching for her waving her flag.

As she climbed up, she could see a lone figure gathering flotsam and jetsam on the shore. The Hermit had already collected a heap of driftwood which had been tossed in by the tide. It would come in useful for building hen-coops or patching pig-stys. Any bits of wood were valuable, for there were only a few stunted trees on the windswept island.

'Yoo-hoo, Mr Skinnymalink!' she called out; but the Hermit took no notice of her. The sea-birds on the other hand, flew up from their perches on the crags with pro-testing cries. Especially when Jinty let out a more piercing shriek. 'There's the boat! He's coming! Mag-nus! Can you see me?'

Jinty waved her flag wildly, then went slithering down the hillside and ran like a hare to join the others at the harbour. They had all turned out, not only to greet Magnus, but to receive their weekly supplies from the mainland. Special treats of sausages, kippers, baker's bread, butcher-meat, fruit, newspapers and mail. Tonight there would be savoury meals being cooked in every cottage kitchen.

'See the bonnie boat,' crooned the District Nurse, shoogling the McCallum twins in her arms. Mrs Gillies had a proprietory interest in them, not only because she had brought them into the world, but because the girl – Rose – had been named after her. They were growing too heavy to carry, but if she set them down they would have crawled straight into the sea. 'See the bonnie boat. Guess who'll be on it!'

Rose and Angus did not bother to guess. They continued to suck their thumbs and watch the bonnie boat, with Captain Campbell at the helm, creaking its way towards the pier.

'There's Magnus!' shrieked Jinty, jumping up and down and waving her flag frantically. 'Yoo-hoo, Magnus! I'm here! Can you see me!'

Magnus could see her all right. Silly wee thing, carrying on like that! All the same, he waved back, carried away by the emotion of the moment. It was great to hear the *Hebridean* bump against the barnacled old pier; great to watch the gang-plank sliding down; great to know that he would soon be stepping on to his native soil.

The Duke was every bit as excited and made no effort to hide his delight. 'I feel years younger already,' he said, jiggling from one foot to another. 'Years and years younger.'

His Grace, indeed, looked almost like a schoolboy, trigged out in shorts and blazer, with a straw boater perched on his head. Magnus, on the other hand, had grown taller and broader, and was wearing a new kilt. At long last he had been forced to discard his Harris tweed, made down from his dead father's Sunday suit. There was still plenty of wear in it even after all those years, but the suit would not be wasted. It would be handed on to another boy. To Tair perhaps. Everything that could be used or worn was communal property in Sula.

Tair – who had been christened Angus Alastair McCallum – had never worn anything new in his life. Only hand-me-downs. Not that he minded, as long as there was a pocket in his trousers. That was the important thing, to have a hiding-place for his best friend, Avizandum.

Avizandum was his familiar, who guided him throughout the day. The two had long conversations, understood by nobody else. Lately, however, there were times when the little creature refused to talk to Tair, and even vanished from his pocket for hours on end.

It was all the fault of Tair's baby brother and sister. Avizandum appeared to be jealous of the attention the boy paid to the twins. Tair spent hours taking them out in their pram and talking to them in childish language. 'Boo-boo! Goo-goo! Moo-moo!'

It was more than Avizandum could stand. No wonder he felt annoyed when Tair stuffed the babies' bibs and bootees into his pocket, leaving precious little room for him.

But today he had no cause for complaint. Tair was paying no attention to the twins. Instead, he was whispering to Avizandum in an excited voice.

'Look, Avizandum, what's that on board the boat? Can you see it?'

'Yes, I can. Wait till I think.'

With a little bit of thinking, Avizandum could always come up with an answer. It did not take him long. 'I know!' he told Tair. 'It's a pony. A wee Shetland pony.'

'Oh my! so it is. Aren't you clever, Avizandum?'

'Yes, I am,' said Avizandum, who did not believe in false modesty.

Tair watched the Shetland pony being coaxed down the gangway with Magnus and the little Duke pushing from behind. It had been His Grace's idea to bring Sheltie to Sula. 'The pony would pine if you left him behind,' he had told Magnus. 'And you'd miss him, too, wouldn't you, boy?'

'Uh-huh!' admitted Magnus. 'So I would.'

Magnus had grown fond of the shaggy little animal who roamed about the castle grounds in company with the dogs and the deer, the wild fox and the peacocks. Sheltie began to follow the boy down the bumpy drive every morning when he set out for the High School. The pony was there again at night, waiting at the gate when Magnus came home.

'Hullo, Sheltie. I'm back.'

As soon as Magnus had opened the gates, the pony was nuzzling at his shoulder. The boy swung his school-bag over his back, took hold of Sheltie's mane and leapt astride. Sheltie kicked up his heels and trotted up the drive to the castle door. It was a kind of shuttle-service which the pony seemed to enjoy.

On most days Magnus walked the two miles from Cronan Castle to the High School. He liked riding the pony in the castle grounds, but not on the main road where the traffic buzzed by like angry bees. In any case, he preferred using his feet. Shank's pony was the best method of propulsion.

Sometimes, if the Duke had things to fetch from the

Cronan shops, he would say, 'Wait, boy; I'll give you a lift in the motor.'

The motor, like everything the Duke possessed, was ancient; and His Grace drove it as if riding a charger. The old gardener had to help him push it out of the tumbledown garage and get rid of the cocks and hens roosting in the back seat. Starting it up was a tricky operation. Sparks flew and smoke bellowed as the engine began to shudder and shake. Then suddenly the car would leap forward like a kangaroo, while the peacocks screamed in alarm and the gardener side-stepped out of its path.

The Duke always dressed for such occasions in special motoring garb. Goggles, Inverness cape, peaked cap with lug-flaps, large leather gloves. His Grace groaned and grunted each time he changed gear and swayed backwards and forwards when going up a hill, as if trying to push the motor forward. The little man had never mastered the art of stopping, let alone starting. When he drew up, it was always with such a jolt that he nearly winded himself against the steering-wheel.

There was never any need for him to blow his horn. The castle motor could be heard long before it was seen, and the people of Cronan took avoiding action, not knowing if the Duke's brakes were in working-order, or if he would bother to slow down when anyone crossed his path.

Sometimes, when he came out of school, Magnus would find the motor back-firing at the gate, and see the Janitor touching his cap to the little Duke. He would jump in and the two would go jolting home together, not saying much, but content in each other's company. When they reached the castle gates, the boy would leap out to open them and let the car through. Sheltie would canter up the drive, running a race with the old motor till it skidded to a standstill at the front door.

It was always a relief to Magnus when the motor was safely pushed into the old garage and left to the mercy of the cocks and hens. He preferred the friendly little pony who seemed to understand every word he said. Already Magnus had drawn dozens of different pictures of Sheltie, rolling in the grass, leaping over a privet-hedge, standing patiently at the castle-gates, kicking up his heels on the lawn.

And now here was Sheltie setting foot on Sula for the first time.

'It's all right, Sheltie. You're safe,' said Magnus, urging him forward.

The pony stumbled on to the shingly beach and raised his head as if sniffing the salty air. Then he nuzzled against Magnus's shoulder, feeling secure as long as the boy was there.

Magnus, too, took a gulp of the good Sula air. Then he exchanged a glance with Gran, enough to see that she was the same as ever. Upright figure, steadfast gaze, wrinkled forehead, a man's cap perched on her steel-grey hair. Gran – the same yesterday, today, and forever.

All was well; he was home.

3 At Home on the Island

Almost before the *Hebridean* had backed out of the pier, Magnus was into his old breeks and off in search of his friend, the seal.

But first he took a critical look at the picture on the wall in Gran's kitchen, where the sheep-dip calendar used to hang. It was the picture he had painted of his father and mother, copied from an old photograph.

The boy stood in front of it as he had stood staring at the paintings in the Art Gallery in Glasgow. His parents seemed to be smiling at him, welcoming him home. It was comforting to see them there; but Magnus was not satisfied with the picture.

'I could do better now,' he told himself.

In the light of the lessons he had learned at the High School, he could see where he had gone wrong. The colouring was crude, there was not enough light and shade, and too little expression on the faces. Yet, imperfect though it was, he knew that Gran looked at it every day as she had never looked at the picture on the sheep-dip calendar. In a way, it was company for her. Her son and his wife were always there in the kitchen, while she was baking scones or scrubbing the floor. He would leave it as it was, without trying to improve it.

There were other pictures he was itching to paint – the colours of Sula. The sea-pinks on the rocks, the burnt-brown bracken on the Heathery Hill, the blood red of a puffin's beak, the smoke-grey peat-reek wisping up to the sky. All the colours were in his paint-box waiting for him to coax them out. But first he must find Old Whiskers.

He fingered the whistle in his pocket, dodged past Jinty and the rest, and ran off to the rocks taking great leaps into the air to release his high spirits. The little Duke, walking with Andrew Murray, the lame schoolmaster, waved his straw hat to him but did not try to detain the boy. He knew where Magnus was going.

Magnus sat on his special rock, playing a few notes on the whistle. Attracted by the sound, a head bobbed up out of the water. 'I'm here!' called Magnus. 'Come on, Old Whiskers. Out on to the rock.'

Old Whiskers gave a happy grunt and heaved himself out of the water. In another moment the two were lying side by side as they had done so often in the past, in complete contentment. Now and again the old seal shifted his body nearer to the boy, afraid that he would disappear again. But gradually as they lay together the fear left him. With a snuffle of satisfaction he relaxed and let the sun seep through his skin.

Magnus himself felt soothed, with a warm-blooded

creature beside him and the familiar sounds of Sula sweeping over him like the Duke's symphony. They were softer than the sounds of Cronan. There, the voices were harsher, the traffic jarred on his ears; even the birds seemed to sing a shriller song. Here, there was nothing louder than the surf swirling against the rocks, the call of the sea-mew, and the bleating of the sheep.

In the distance he could hear the children chattering to each other as they took turns to ride the Shetland pony. Already Sheltie had become a communal plaything. He was a patient enough beast and allowed the Ferret to slither on and off his back like a cowboy. Jinty tried to sit sideways like a fine lady, but it was not easy without a saddle. Tair had difficulty in getting on, but none in getting off. He took a dozen tumbles in his stride; and Black Sandy and Red Sandy tried to ride the pony together, till Sheltie shook them all off and trotted away to graze beside the sheep on the Heathery Hill.

Magnus continued to lie beside the seal in a blissful daze, shutting out from his mind all thoughts of the past and the future. He felt like a Willy Wisp hovering in mid-air.

Jinty Cowan was hovering, too, but not in mid-air. She was watching and waiting at a safe distance ready to pounce on Magnus the moment he stirred. She was knitting to pass the time. It was a new skill she had recently acquired, and Jinty was putting her heart and soul into it. Purl and plain, as fast as could be, and never mind the dropped stitches.

'See!' she cried to anyone who would look. 'I've done all this since breakfast.'

Jinty longed above everything else for recognition. It was not enough that she admired herself. She wanted others to do the same. Especially Magnus.

Today she was knitting him a scarf – a long blue woolly comforter called a gravat. It was pale blue – for a boy – and grubby in patches where the wool had dropped on the ground. Jinty did not believe in sitting knitting at home, hiding her light under a bushel. She tucked the wool under her arm and walked about while she purled and plained. Sometimes, in the stress of starting a new row, the ball would slip from its moorings and roll in the mud; but Jinty just picked it up, rubbed it on her skirt, and went on knitting.

The Reverend Alexander Morrison was approaching her. Jinty brightened up and knitted faster. The minister was sure to notice her and say something complimentary. He would be sure to say something, anyway, for he was a jokey man, always ready with his quips and jests. Anything for a laugh.

'Knit! Knit! Knit!' he said, putting on a comical face. 'What's the hurry? Are you trying to get it finished before the wool runs out?'

The minister laughed at his own wit, while Jinty held up the knitting to show him. Look, Mr Morrison, I've done all this ...' But the minister was finished with the subject, and with his wee jokes. He had other matters on his mind.

'Did you hear about the excursion?' he asked.

Little Miss Know-All would have liked to say 'Yes,' but she was forced to say 'No.' The word *excursion* puzzled her. What could it mean?

'An outing,' said Mr Morrison, as if reading her thoughts. 'There'll be a whole boat-load coming from Cronan for the day. Captain Campbell from the *Hebridean* was telling me about it, and asking if I could organize some entertainment. Games and sports and things.'

He squared his shoulders as if ready to organise anything from a cricket-match to a coronation. Jinty felt flattered that the minister was confiding in her, especially when he went on to say, 'I was thinking we might have some music and dancing. You're good at the Highland Fling, aren't you, Jinty?'

'Oh yes, I am,' agreed Jinty. Her eyes shone at the prospect of pirouetting in front of a boat-load of tourists. Maybe there would be a film-producer or a theatre-manager amongst them. She would be discovered! MISS JINTY COWAN. Her name would be up in lights, and she would have two mink coats and a dozen diamond rings.

'I can do the Sword Dance as well,' she told the minister. There were no swords in Sula, but she could make do with the poker and tongs. 'And reels, too,' she added for good measure. There was no end to her talents.

'Well, then,' said the minister, as if that was one item settled. 'I'll be making an announcement in the church on Sunday.' And off he went mumbling to himself as he planned the rest of the programme.

Jinty could not wait till Sunday to make her own announcement. Bursting with excitement, she threw caution – and her knitting – to the wind, and ran helter-skelter to tell Magnus the great news.

'Oh, Magnus, d'you know what? There's to be an excursion from Cronan. A whole boat-load of trippers coming here for the day. There's to be games and sports and everything. Fancy that! I'm to entertain them with my dancing. I'll wear my new tartan frock with the velvet ribbons. It's awful exciting, isn't it not?'

'No!'

It was the last thing Magnus wanted to hear. A boat-load of trippers coming to disturb his peace! Indeed, his peace was already disturbed, for at the sound of Jinty's piping voice, Old Whiskers had slithered off the rock and flopped back into the sea. The moment of bliss was gone for ever.

'You're a silly wee thing!' he burst out, pushing past Jinty and rushing off towards the Heathery Hill. Rory the collie-dog got up from old Cowan's doorstep and came scampering after him, panting with pleasure to have the boy back on the island again.

'Good old dog,' said Magnus, stooping to pat him. Animals, in his opinion, had more sense than silly lasses like Jinty Cowan.

Sheltie was slithering about on the lower slopes, trying to find his feet on the rough ground. Trying, too, to find a mouthful of fresh grass to crop amongst the clumps of heather and bracken. It was a great deal sparser here than in the overgrown wilderness around Cronan Castle. All the same, the pony seemed to be enjoying a few tasty bites, and was content enough in his new surroundings. Especially when he saw the familiar figure of Magnus coming towards him.

The pony threw up his head and made to follow the boy, but Magnus gave him a friendly push in passing and said, 'No, Sheltie. Stay where you are. I'm going right up.'

As he climbed higher with the dog at his heels, Magnus stopped now and then to look at his favourite scene. The whole island was spread out beneath him like a living map, with Little Sula to the west and nothing except miles and miles of open sea.

He could see the children playing at the harbour, Gran stumping out to feed the hens, the District Nurse riding her wobbly bicycle, and old Cowan leaning on his crook staring at his sheep. Everything was exactly as Magnus had pictured it during his exile on the mainland, It was wonderful to be back and to find that nothing had changed.

He went on round the brow of the hill where the Hermit, having finished his task of gathering driftwood was sitting patiently polishing away at his stones.

'Hullo, Mr Skinnymalink,' said the boy, flinging himself down at the Hermit's side.

'Hullo, Magnus,' said the Hermit in his croaky voice. He did not look up or make any other comment. They had greeted each other and that was enough.

A long silence. Then Magnus pointed to one of the stones lying at the Hermit's side. 'There's one like that in Glasgow,' the boy told him. 'In the Museum. It's in a glass case with a label on it.'

'M'm!'

It was enough for Mr Skinnymalink to find the stones and polish them till the hidden colours began to sparkle. What happened to them afterwards did not matter to him. All the same, he noted the information and continued to polish all the harder.

Suddenly he looked up at Magnus and said, 'I'm glad you're back.'

'Me, too,' said Magnus and gave a sigh of satisfaction. It was as if the two had shaken hands.

*

Specky the hen was pecking about on Gran's well-scrubbed kitchen floor, seeking what she could find. She was a communal bird, popping in at any open door and laying her eggs wherever she happened to settle down, often on the old rag rug in front of Gran's peat-fire.

'Help yourself,' said Magnus, dropping a few crumbs of oatcake for her benefit. He had finished his supper and had a comfortable feeling in his inside. No one could make such tasty stovies as Gran. He would have liked to say thank you to her for the good food. He tried, but the words stuck in his throat. He was not sure how she would take it.

Gran was lighting the lamp, turning up the wick slowly so that the sudden heat would not crack the glass globe. A warm glow spread over the kitchen softening the shabby corners and showing up the picture of his father and mother. It was a kindlier light than the bright 'electric' on the mainland.

Magnus leant back in his hard chair feeling at peace with the world. He had a small bruise on his forehead, the result of his first fight with the Ferret. It had been one of their usual tussles, half in fun, half in earnest. It was great being able to use his fists again. There was no one at the High School worth fighting, though now and again he had a brush with a bully if he found him pestering Wee Willy. But he and the Ferret had their own way of fighting. It was all part of their special feeling for each other.

'Mag-nus!'

Gran was not one for letting him sit idle for long, even on his first night home. She gave him a sharp look and asked, 'Have you shut in the hens?'

'Uh-huh!'

'And fed the cow?'

'Uh-huh!'

'What about the peat?'

'It's in.'

'Then you'd better take this to the schoolhouse.'

She was packing food into a basket, as she so often did: scones, butter, cheese, a pot of raspberry jam. Finally, she poured some milk into a can and said, 'The schoolmaster'll be needing extra, with the Duke staying there. Take it, Magnus.'

There was no disobeying Gran when she gave an order. Magnus took the basket and the can, and went out into the gloaming. The night air had become thin and sharp, like soor-dook. He could hear sleepy sounds from the birds nesting on the rocks, and the steady lapping of the water against the boats moored on the shore. Jinty was hovering in the lamp-lit lobby of the General Store next door, knitting away for dear life.

'Oh hullo, Magnus, are you coming in?' she asked, ever hopeful that a miracle might happen.

'No, I'm not,' said Magnus, marching on.

'I'm knitting a gravat for you,' she called after him. 'Maybe you'll come in on your way back.'

'Maybe,' said Magnus; but it was a very doubtful maybe.

When he reached the schoolhouse, he hung back, not wanting to go in and face the schoolmaster. It was Mr Murray who had urged him in the first place to go to the High School. Likely the man would be wanting to know how he had got on, and if he was going back for another term. It was something Magnus did not want to talk about. Indeed, he did not want to talk about anything. He would just say 'Hullo,' dump the food, and run back home.

He looked through the window and saw two men sitting at the table, poring over the draught-board. The Duke and Mr Skinnymalink. It was not often that the Hermit left his cave on the hillside or the lonely hut where he spent his nights; but the schoolhouse door was always open to him. Now and again he would wander in, especially if the little Duke was there. The two would sit for hours in silence, planning out each move of the game as if it was an army manœuvre. They looked like a still-life picture, sitting there hardly moving a muscle.

The lame schoolteacher, looking frailer than usual, was by the fire with his little dog, Trix, on the rug at his feet. Andrew Murray was writing in an exercise-book. Correcting the children's essays, maybe.

When Magnus went in, the two men at the table came to life. The Hermit turned round with a startled look, but relaxed when he saw it was only Magnus. The little Duke beamed at him, waved his hand and cried, 'Hullo, boy. Everything all right?'

'Yes, it's okay,' said Magnus.

He gave a sidelong glance at the schoolmaster who laid aside the exercise-book and said warmly, 'Come in and sit down, Magnus.'

Magnus drew back, like an animal not wanting to be trapped. 'I'm not staying,' he mumbled. 'I just brought some stuff from Gran.'

'Thank you, Magnus. Wait till I empty the basket.' Andrew Murray got up, dragging his lame leg, and took away the food, while Magnus stood by the table watching the two men at their game.

'It's years since I've enjoyed such a good game as this,' said the little Duke. 'Years and years. Your move, Mr Skinnymalink.'

Mr Skinnymalink was not to be hurried. He sat as immovable as a rock, keeping his eyes fixed unblinkingly on the board, pondering for a long time before his hand hovered above the counters. But the move he made was the right one, and he sank back in his seat with a look of satisfaction on his face.

'By jove!' exploded the Duke, clutching his brow in mock despair. 'You've got me cornered. I'm done for!' He peered at the board. 'No, I'm not! Wait! Let me think. There might be a way out.'

He lapsed into silence, and Magnus would have taken his leave if the little dog had not suddenly stood on her hindlegs, like a performing animal, asking to be petted. She looked so appealing that Magnus stooped down and swept the small bundle up into his arms. She was a soft creature, more like a toy than a real dog, but Magnus found it difficult to resist her quivering little barks and bites.

'Silly wee thing!' he said, cradling her in his arms.

Andrew Murray saw that the dog might succeed where he had failed in detaining Magnus. But he was wise enough not to question the boy about the High School. Instead, he went back to his chair by the fire and began turning over the pages of the exercise-book.

'I wonder if I've got this right?' he said in a casual voice to nobody in particular. 'It's about Sula. I'm trying to write a book about the seals and the wildlife, and about the people and their way of living. I've been hearing strange stories about the Fairy Ring on Little Sula.'

Magnus said nothing. He laid down the little dog and looked coldly at the teacher. The man was an incomer. What would he know about the seals and the Fairy Ring? Let him stick to his arithmetic.

The Duke, however, looked up from his game and said: 'Stories? What stories? Tell us.'

Magnus was half-way to the door when the schoolmaster began to read what he had written in the exercise-book. It was an old tale he had heard from one of the islanders.

'One dark night a strange light could be seen flickering on Little Sula. Who could be there? Was it a will-o'-the-wisp? Or a pirate? Or perhaps a ghost?'

Magnus had heard the tale before, but never as well-told. The people of Sula believed that wishes – especially evil wishes – could come true if made inside the Fairy Ring on the island. There had been stories about sheep and cattle dying, people falling sick, or even drowning because of someone ill-wishing them. But they were just old tales. All the same, Magnus was careful himself to think only good thoughts whenever he stepped inside that strange green circle on Little Sula. It was best to be on the safe side.

Andrew Murray brought the tale to life so vividly that even the Hermit looked up from the draught-board to listen. Magnus, too, was so absorbed that he stood still, forgetting that he had been about to make his escape.

As for the little Duke, when the schoolmaster paused at the end of the story, he cried out: 'Go on, man! Tell us some more.'

Andrew Murray turned over the pages and read snatches of what he had written about the seals, the peat-gathering, the crofts, the fishing, and the close-knit life of the people of Sula.

As the man continued to read, Magnus began to see pictures. The young seals tumbling over each other in the water. The Merry Dancers streaking across the night sky. The fishing boats rounding Sula Point in a storm. Rory chasing after the sheep on the Heathery Hill. Vignettes of crabs, jellyfish, sea-shells, scarlet rowan-berries, stone dykes, and purple heather-bells all flashed before the boy's eyes. As he stood there listening, he was illustrating the book.

The schoolmaster paused in his reading and looked up at him. He had the same thought in his mind, but he had enough sense not to voice it. As he laid the book aside he said casually, 'Of course, these are only words.'

'Uh-huh!' said Magnus, without realising he was speaking. He knew what the schoolmaster meant. Maybe he would get busy with his pencils and paints, and bring the words to life. But he was not going to let the teacher know.

'I'm away!' he said suddenly, and darted out of the door.

Outside, he heard a sudden strange honking in the air. Looking up he saw a sight that filled his heart with delight, better than all the still-life pictures in the world. A flock of wild swans, their long necks out-stretched, were flying across the night sky towards Little Sula. Sometimes they found their way there, to feed – like Gran's sheep – on the fresh green grass. Would they wish any wishes, he wondered, if they stepped inside the Fairy Ring?

Another sound near by startled him.

'Pssst!'

A furtive figure was lurking near the schoolhouse. The Ferret bent on mischief.

'What's up?' asked Magnus suspiciously.

'Here, Magnus; hold that.'

'What is it?'

'String,' said the Ferret, thrusting it into Magnus's hand. 'You hold one end. I'm going to hold the other, once I've stretched it across the road.'

'What for?' asked Magnus cautiously.

'Mrs Gillies. Look! She's coming on her bicycle,' said the Ferret, chuckling at his cleverness. 'She'll never see the string.' It would be fun to topple the District Nurse into the ditch and send her bicycle spinning. Magnus could see the light from her bicycle-lamp bobbing up and down as she came spinning along the rough road towards them.

'You're a cruel beast,' he burst out at the Ferret, and let go the string. 'I'll punch your nose for you.'

'You're a muckle softie, that's what you are, Magnus Macduff,' roared the Ferret, furious at having been done out of his fun. 'I'll murder you!'

He rushed across the road, and by the time Mrs Gillies reached them, the two boys were locked in a deadly battle. She rang her bell sharply and called, 'Are you two at it again! Get out of the way or you'll get run over.'

Magnus stepped aside but still kept hold of the Ferret by the throat. 'What's up?' he called after her, for it was unusual to see the District Nurse out and about at such an hour, unless sudden illness had struck one of the islanders.

Mrs Gillies was always delighted when her services were called upon. The people of Sula were far too healthy for her liking, leaving her little to do except deal with styes in the eyes, cut knees, or an occasional burn or bruise. But tonight it was something more serious.

'Whooping-cough,' she called out. But there was not the usual note of satisfaction in her voice as she said it.

Magnus could tell that she was worried. 'It's the twins. It came on suddenly; and they're very bad. Especially Rose. She's got a high fever. I'll have a job to pull her through.'

She went cycling off in the darkness towards the McCallums' cottage, leaving Magnus with a blank feeling in his heart.

'Let go,' he said, giving the Ferret a push away from him. His sparring-partner was ready for another bout of in-fighting, but Magnus had lost the notion. He picked up the basket and milk-can and hurried home, trying to dodge past the Cowans' door before Jinty could accost him.

He was not quick enough.

'Come on in, Magnus,' pleaded Jinty. 'We could play the grammyphone ...'

'No, thanks.'

He was in no mood to hear *Over The Sea To Skye* played on the Cowans' wheezy gramophone, or to listen to Jinty's chatter. He scurried past her and went into Gran's cottage, calling out: 'Gran! did you know that the twins are ill?'

Gran knew. She was not in. Magnus guessed, as he looked round the empty kitchen, where she would be. At the McCallums' helping the District Nurse to minister to the sick children.

Though Gran looked so grim and forbidding, there was no one in Sula readier to lend a hand in time of trouble, and none with more experience of life and death. Magnus felt a little easier in his mind, but he could not settle to do any odd jobs in the kitchen. Besides, Gran had already washed up and left everything neat and tidy. He put another lump of peat on the fire, and pushed the kettle nearer to keep it on the boil. Then he lit his little bedroom lamp and carried it upstairs.

He had no thought of going to sleep. For a time he sat on the bed thinking of little Rose and her high fever. What could he do to help? Maybe he could go across to Little Sula and wish a wish in the Fairy Ring.

Suddenly he caught sight of his drawing-materials. The lamplight was too dim for him to use his paints, but at least he could rough-out some of the images that were still whirling through his head, sparked off by the schoolmaster's tales.

4 Sunday in Sula

Magnus set to work to draw the scenes he loved so well. Old Whiskers sunning himself on the rock: a flurry of sea-birds following the *Hebridean* into the harbour: the rowan-tree bending in the breeze in the Manse garden: the wild swans streaking across the sky to Little Sula: a black-faced sheep standing in the middle of the Fairy Ring.

At last the lamp gave a flicker and went out. A shaft of moonlight beamed in through the window. It was not bright enough for Magnus to continue his work, but bright enough for him to see, as he looked out, a lonely figure wandering about on the beach. The moonbeams made a silvery pathway on the water, and everything looked still and peaceful, except for a small restless boy pacing up and down. Tair! What was he doing out there, all by himself, and long past his bedtime?

Tair was not alone. Avizandum was with him, tucked up in his pocket. Indeed, it had been Avizandum who had led Tair out of the McCallums' house away from the distressing sounds of cough-cough-coughing.

'Come on outside,' he urged Tair. 'Let's go for a walk. Maybe the twins'll be better by the time we come back.'

'Oh, d'you think so, Avizandum?' asked Tair, clutching at straws. 'I'm awful worried about them.'

'Me, too,' admitted Avizandum.

Strangely enough, now that the twins were so ill, Avizandum's jealousy seemed to have vanished. He had become his old talkative self, doing his best to comfort young Tair who had been hovering at the sickroom door.

'Wee Rose isn't going to die, is she?' asked Tair fearfully.

For once Avizandum did not give him a direct answer. He stirred uneasily in the boy's pocket and said, 'Come for a walk. It'll be better away from the house.'

It was better in some ways to be outside, away from the moaning and coughing of the sick children. Better to be walking in the moonlight with Avizandum in his pocket to comfort him. But Tair's heart was heavy when he thought of Rose with her chubby cheeks and her infectious little giggle. What if he was never to hear it again?

'She was just beginning to speak,' he told Avizandum as he wandered aimlessly along the beach. 'She was quicker than Angus. She could say da-da and ta-ta and puff-puff.'

The lump in his throat grew bigger when he realized he was speaking of Rose in the past tense. Tears began to trickle down his cheeks, and he started to sob as if his heart would break.

'Wheesht!' said Avizandum suddenly. 'Wheesht, Tair! Keep quiet.'

Tair swallowed his sobs and wiped away the tears with his knuckles. 'What's up?' he asked, trembling all over. 'Has something happened?'

'Yes, yes! Something's happened!' The little creature seemed to be jumping about in Tair's pocket. 'It's okay, Tair! Okay!'

'What?' cried Tair, standing stock-still at the edge of the sea. 'D'you mean they're going to get better? Rose, too?'

'Rose, too!' Avizandum assured him in a delighted voice. 'They've got the turn. Isn't it great?'

Great! It was such good news that Tair did not know how to contain himself. He could not make up his mind whether to run straight into the sea or turn somersaults on the shingly beach. Instead, he took a great jump for joy into the air and shouted: 'Hooray!' at the pitch of his voice.

It was then that Magnus Macduff came hurrying towards him.

'Tair,' he cried. 'What are you doing out here?'

'Oh, Magnus, the twins are going to get better. Avizandum says so,' said Tair, still jumping for joy.

'That's good,' said Magnus, though he was less sure of Avizandum's powers. 'Come on; I'll take you home.'

As they neared the McCallums' cottage they saw the District Nurse's bicycle propped up at the side of the door. Gran was coming out, hitching her shawl over her head against the cool night air. She looked weary but satisfied.

'They'll pull through,' she said briefly, and left it at that; but it was enough.

'I told you!' said Tair triumphantly. 'Avizandum's never wrong.'

He dashed inside, while Magnus and Gran walked silently home side by side. In the moonlight the boy could see, as he stole a glance at her, that her step was slower and her back more bent. With a stab at his heart he realized that Gran was growing older.

He would have liked to take her arm and say, 'Lean on me, Gran.' Instead, as they neared their own door-step, he told her. 'The kettle's boiling. I'll make you a cup of tea.'

The sentiment seemed to get through. Gran's step grew lighter, her back straighter. She gave a little sigh and said, 'That's good, laddie. I could do with a cup.'

*

It was a special day in Sula. Sunday – the Sabbath Day.

'I have the following announcements to make,' said the Reverend Alexander Morrison, standing up in the pulpit, a godly figure in gown and dog-collar. Very different from the man who dug the Manse garden on weekdays and made comic remarks to everyone passing by. Today he was no ordinary human being. He was one of the Lord's chosen people, set up above the rest of the congregation to show them the errors of their ways. He was their direct link between heaven and hell.

From his vantage-point in the pulpit he could keep a stern eye on his flock. They were all there, with the exception of Mr Skinnymalink who was hovering about outside, and Mrs McCallum who was at home nursing the twins. Even old Morag McLeod, with her varicose veins, had been helped into the back pew where she sat hunched up, with an extra-strong peppermint in her pocket in case she should be overcome by an attack of wind in the stomach.

Like the preacher himself, the congregation all looked different today. They were ill-at-ease in their Sunday clothes. Old Cowan, wearing his good black suit, was acting as beadle. It was an important office, first in command after the minister himself. Apart from ringing the bell, his chief duty was to march solemnly in with the Good Book – the big bible – carry it up the pulpit steps, and open it at Exodus, or wherever His Reverence was going to read.

After a glance round the church, he descended the stairs at a steady tread, and disappeared into the vestry. After a decent interval, he came back leading in the minister, as if Mr Morrison could not find his own way. Then, after shutting him up in the pulpit, he went and sat beside the Cowans in their pew. Only now could the service begin.

'Look, Tair! Watch Mrs Gillies. Isn't she funny?'

No one heard the whisper except Tair. The service would have been dull and dreary for him if it had not been for the small creature hiding in his pocket. Avizandum was in no way awed by such solemn surroundings, and could always find something to tickle his funny-bone and to keep Tair in constant fits of the giggles.

'Watch her,' he repeated, during the singing of a psalm. 'She looks as if she's riding her bicycle.'

True enough, the District Nurse who was playing the organ, seemed to be pedalling away as if she was in a hurry to get to heaven. It was a Psalm: 'I To The Hills Will Lift Mine Eyes.' Mrs Gillies was putting her heart and soul, as well as her feet, into it, though her left hand did not always know what her right was doing. Her playing was loud, if nothing else. The little Duke, sitting in the schoolmaster's pew, winced at the discords and turned his eyes to the ceiling instead of to the hills.

Mrs Gillies liked a rousing hymn best of all. *Onward Christian Soldiers* was her favourite. She could get up a great speed with it, and feel fully-stretched for once.

It was not so long since the organ had been installed in the little church. Some of the older members of the congregation did not approve of such a noisy instrument. The *kist o' whustles*, they called it. They preferred the old custom of having a man to lead the praise. A precentor. In earlier days, old Cowan had stood up in front of them, thumping his tuning-fork on his knee to find the right note, before leading them through the maze of psalms and paraphrases. It was a more seemly way, they felt, of praising the Lord than disturbing the Sabbath peace with a wheezy kist o' whustles.

Old Cowan kept the tuning-fork in his pocket in the hope that either the organ or Mrs Gillies would break down but the 'machine' kept going, and the District Nurse pedalled bravely on, like a Christian soldier.

'The Bible-class will meet in the Manse on Wednesday evening at seven sharp,' said the minister, looking over his spectacles at his parishioners. Then, mingling the secular with the sacred, he told them, 'There will be an excursion from Cronan next week.' He had little need to announce it, for it was a well-known fact by now, which had been discussed inside-out on every doorstep.

'Help will be needed to provide the tea, and to run the

sports and entertainment. Those willing to assist should get in touch with me as soon as possible.' The minister changed his tone and added, 'The offering will now be received.'

Hands went into pockets and purses as Angus McCallum, Tair's father, left his seat and went round with the collection plate. Mrs Gillies played a bright piece on the organ while the harvest was gathered in. The Lord loveth a cheerful giver.

The diversion over, the people settled back in their pews to endure the long sermon as best they could. Mr Morrison gave them their money's worth and never preached for less than an hour. It seemed more like a year to some of the younger members of the congregation.

Magnus gazed ahead of him at the stained-glass window. The sun was streaming through, lighting up the dark blues, purples and reds of the picture. It was a strange picture, Magnus thought; though he was so used to it by now that he scarcely noticed it. Like Gran's aspidistra, or the old tin bath lying in Cowan's field, it was always there.

The picture showed the Good Shepherd, wearing a long nightgown and carrying a lamb under his arm. In his hand he held a long crook, like old Cowan's. A group of small children were huddled at his feet, also dressed in nightgowns. Underneath were the words: SUFFER THE LITTLE CHILDREN TO COME UNTO ME.

Magnus was not sure who was suffering. The children or the Good Shepherd? The Bible was full of puzzles, but he liked many of its rolling phrases. Great mouthfuls of words. 'Verily, verily, I say unto you.'

His own Bible, lying on the edge of the pew, had once belonged to his father. *Magnus Macduff* was written on the fly-leaf in a stiff hand. His father had been no better scribe than himself. A sad postscript had been added by Gran. *Died 23 February 1962.*

It was the only book of Magnus's in which he had not scrawled any pictures round the margins, though he often had an urge to depict all the biblical animals: the ox and the ass, the donkey in the stable, the lions in their den, and all the creatures entering the Ark, two by two. But the Bible was a sacred book, and the kirk was no place for drawing pictures. Besides, Gran, sitting stiff and straight as a poker beside him, would have stunned him with a look. There were strict rules to be obeyed in the church, and one of them was to sit still and pretend that everyday things did not exist.

Sunday seemed a long dreary day in Sula, especially for the young people. They were expected to curb their high spirits, as if turning off a switch, put childish things behind them and suddenly become as sedate as grown-ups. No playing games; no running or shouting; no whistling. It was a sin even to smile on the Sabbath day. *Suffer the little children.*

The curtains and blinds in all the windows were drawn, so that even the houses looked lifeless. Only the most essential work could be done. The cows could be milked and the animals fed; but there was to be no cooking or washing or fishing or peat-gathering. All life came to a standstill.

It was strange how the animals seemed to sense the difference. Rory never barked. Cowan's goat walked about as sedately as an old-age pensioner. Even the sheep bleated in a lower key and the sea-gulls floated more gently on the air, stifling their raucous cries. Only Sheltie, a newcomer to Sula, broke the rules and kicked up his

59

heels on the Heathery Hill with as much abandon as if it was a week-day.

'O dear!' sighed Tair during the sermon. 'I wish it was over. I'm fed up. What are you doing, Avizandum?'

'Sleeping,' came a voice from his pocket. 'Wheesht!'

Morag McLeod was sleeping, too, in the back pew with a half-sucked peppermint in her mouth. Old Cowan had his eyes wide open but there was a dazed look in them. The rest seemed to have turned to stone. The sermon was an endurance test for both old and young, though the grown-ups knew better how to hide their feelings. If they were listening, they could tell by the preacher's headings – firstly, secondly, thirdly, and finally – when the Amen was in sight. But it was a long time coming.

The Ferret, a restless laddie at the best of times, felt the strain more than any. Jinty could console herself with Dolly Mixtures popped into her mouth under cover of her hand, or she could take little keeks at Magnus to see if he was admiring her pink straw hat. Tair had Avizandum for company. Black Sandy and Red Sandy had a private game, making faces at each other; but the Ferret was at a loose end. His catapult had been confiscated for the day, and he was bereft of all enjoyment. If he had been near Magnus they could have had a punch-up below the pew, but they were seated several rows apart.

The Ferret had been given one sweet – a pandrop – to last him throughout the sermon. It was little enough consolation. If he crunched it with his teeth, it was gone in one gulp. Even if he sucked it, the minister had hardly got started before the pandrop was gone beyond recall. After that, there was nothing left to hope for.

Magnus did not find the strain so great. He just sat

and thought. As the Reverend Alexander Morrison's voice boomed from the pulpit, he gazed at the Good Shepherd and wondered about the other Magnus Macduff who had sat in the same pew. What had he thought about? The fishing, maybe. Or the seals. Gran had said, in one of her rare bursts of confidence, that his father had been fond of the birds and beasts. The seals most of all. Like father like son.

'Secondly, my dear brethren ...'

It was strange to think on Sunday everyone was the minister's brother. Even old Morag McLeod. He was well into his stride by now, waving his arms like flails, spouting about heaven and hell as if he knew them both intimately. Mr Morrison liked hearing the sound of his own voice. If no one else enjoyed the sermon, he did.

Driven to desperation, the Ferret began to do his exploding act, holding his breath till he grew scarlet in the face, then letting it out like a steam-engine. Magnus watched him, knowing that he would not get away with it for long. Sure enough, old Cowan birled round in his seat and gave the boy a stern look that spoke louder than words. The Ferret subsided, all the steam taken out of him, and began to count his fingers for lack of anything better to do.

Magnus felt a stab of sympathy for the restless redheaded boy. Had old Cowan never wriggled about with boredom when he was young? How soon they forget, the grown-ups. Magnus stole a glance at Gran and wondered about her in her young days. Had she ever played games? Somehow he could not imagine Gran bowling a hoop, jumping over a skipping-rope, or singing 'One-two-three-a-leerie'.

The little Duke, at least, was human enough not to

disguise his feelings. He kept drumming his fingers on the ledge of the pew, playing a little tune to himself. Now and again he turned his head and winked at Magnus, who tried hard to keep a poker-face. His Grace's sigh of relief was louder than any when the minister finally said 'Amen'.

There was a great rustling and coughing amongst the congregation and a loud singing of the last psalm, as they all gave way to their pent-up feelings. It was a great release to be making a noise.

The Duke sang a descant of his own, making it up as the spirit moved him. Some swayed backwards and forwards, keeping up a kind of rhythm. Others held their psalm-books in their hands but never looked at them, letting it be seen that they knew the words off by heart. The District Nurse pulled out every stop and pedalled triumphantly to the end.

The minister blessed them, and old Cowan let him out of the pulpit while the congregation sat with bowed heads saying their last prayers. Or, more likely, thinking of their dinners. Then the church door was opened, and a welcome breath of fresh air blew in, reviving everyone's flagging spirits.

The Ferret was the first to rush out, taking a great leap into the air through sheer relief. He would have jumped over the grave-stones and challenged Magnus to a wrestling-match if the grown-ups had not been watching.

Magnus inhaled a lungful of air, feeling the same sense of release as he did every time he emerged from the grim High School at Cronan. Sometimes, when school was over he ran down to the harbour to take a longing look at the *Hebridean*, his only link with home.

He would have leapt on board, if it had not been for the thought of the Duke.

'Stick it out, boy; stick it out!' the little man kept urging him. 'You're learning. You're getting somewhere.'

Where? Surely there could be no better place in the world than Sula, even on a solemn Sunday, with the peesweeps calling overhead and the white waves rustling in to the shore, quiet, peaceful, unchanging.

Not so peaceful!

Suddenly a strange thing happened which made everyone stop in their tracks and blink their eyes, not believing what they saw. Mr Skinnymalink was running towards them waving his arms wildly and shouting in his hoarse voice. It was so surprising to see the Hermit behaving in such a manner, in full view of everyone, that they were all too dumbfounded to make a move. Except Magnus, who ran forward to meet him.

'What's up, Mr Skinnymalink?' he called out anxiously.

'Twins!' shouted the Hermit, waving his skinny arms. 'Twins!'

Magnus's heart missed a beat. Rose and Angus! Had something happened to them? 'Are they worse?' he cried out.

The Hermit mopped his brow and croaked, 'Worse! No, no; they're fine, both of them. Tibby's all right, too.'

'Tibby!' cried Gran, hurrying forward, clutching her bible. 'Has the cow calved already? She wasn't due till the middle of the week. On the Sabbath, too!' She took an anxious look at the Hermit. 'How did you manage?'

'All right,' he said, still flushed with his achievement. 'The calves are up on their feet already.'

'Well done, Mr Skinnymalink,' cried Magnus. 'Come on; let's go and look at them.'

But the Hermit drew back. The first flush of excitement was fading now that he saw himself the centre of attraction with the islanders all crowding round him. Dressed, too, in their Sunday clothes, while he was shabbier than a scarecrow. Without another word he turned away and loped off to his refuge on the Heathery Hill. He had brought two new lives into the world while the others were worshipping. It would be something to think about as he sat polishing his stones in the cave.

Everyone, even the minister, trooped to the little byre where Gran's cow was lying contentedly on the hay watching her newly-born calves trying out their shaky legs. Sometimes they tumbled down, but bravely struggled up again, determined to find their feet.

'Not bad,' said old Cowan, looking at them closely. 'They'll grow into fine beasts.'

Gran, too, looked satisfied. After all, it was a great thing for her to have two healthy new animals to add to her small stock. But all she said was, 'They'll do.'

Magnus watched them nuzzling against their mother, and marvelled at their ability to get to grips with life so quickly. Unlike helpless humans who took so long to stand on their own feet.

A sudden feeling of pure happiness came over him. The reason for it was all mixed up. It had to do with his being back home in Sula, that the McCallum twins were out of danger, that Tibby had produced two calves, and that he had a new picture of them to draw. He let out a light-hearted whistle, then clapped his hand to his mouth to stifle it when the minister frowned on him.

'Magnus Macduff, remember this is the Sabbath day,'

His Reverence told him reproachfully. It was bad enough that Tibby had forgotten herself, but he was not going to have the rest of his flock straying from the straight and narrow path.

'We'll need to christen the wee calves,' said Jinty; as if, with the minister present, the time was ripe. She sidled up to Magnus, hoping – for she would never learn sense – that he might say, 'We could call them Jinty and Magnus,' but naturally he said nothing. They were Gran's calves, and if they needed names, she would do the christening.

Jinty was in no way cast down. Indeed, there was an elevated air about her, as if she was dying to blurt out a secret. And so she was!

Jinty had had a vision in church. Not a holy vision like the one on the way to Damascus. This was a more worldly flash of light; but it was a flash all the same. During the sermon her busy brain had been working overtime. The result was the most wonderful plot she had ever concocted. If only she could carry it out! She must be very cautious, very subtle.

It was a great idea. Brilliant! She would have to get Mr Murray, the schoolmaster, to arrange it. After all, she was clever enough. Far cleverer than any of the other pupils in the island school. It was time she moved on to higher things. To the Girls' High School in Cronan, in fact.

The attraction, of course, was Magnus. She saw herself smartly-dressed in her school uniform, walking by his side while he proudly carried her schoolbag. If she played her cards well, maybe the Duke would invite her to stay in the castle. Miss Jinty Cowan of Cronan Castle. If not, she could still go to Cronan and live with her cousins, the

Reekies at Rockview. It was all cut and dried in her mind long before the minister reached 'Finally'. The service had not been wasted on Jinty.

'You've got brains,' she told herself smugly, hugging her secret to herself. 'You're not daft, Jinty Cowan!'

5 The Excursion

'In-out! In-out!'

Magnus was rowing two passengers across to Little
Sula. The Hermit, and one of Gran's black-faced sheep.
The Hermit was seeking refuge, and the ewe was being
taken there for a change of pasture.

The bobbing seals followed in the wake of the boat,
turning head-over-tail like frisky children. Old Whiskers
ploughed a steadier course, puffing and blowing as he
tried to keep up with the others. He was not so nimble

nowadays. All he wanted was to lie in peace on the rock with the boy at his side.

Peace! There was little enough peace in Sula today – the day of the excursion.

All the islanders were on the go, hurrying to get through their work so that they would be free to entertain the trippers when they arrived. All except Mr Skinnymalink. The thought of the invasion was too much for him.

'I can't stand it,' he told Magnus in his croaky voice. Sometimes he did not speak for hours, even days; and when he did, he sounded as rusty as an old tin can. 'Take me across to Little Sula. I'll stay there till they've all gone.'

'Right,' said Magnus, without making any fuss. No one understood the Hermit's feelings better than he did. Except Gran, maybe. The old woman hated having her peace shattered by noisy strangers rampaging over the island, chasing the sheep, poking into hen-houses, and wanting her to pose for 'snaps' beside the peat-stack. They left gates open, litter lying about, and caused such confusion that it would be days before everything was back to normal and the hens started laying again.

Her hospitable instincts were too strong for her to ignore the excursion altogether. She had been up at the crack of dawn baking a great batch of scones, pancakes, shortbread, and oatcakes, now cooling on wire trays on the kitchen table. Before Magnus left for Little Sula she buttered some of the scones, cut off a hunk of cheese, and filled a flask with tea.

'That'll see him through the day,' she said, putting the food into a basket and handing it to Magnus. Gran always referred to the Hermit as *him*. 'Tell him he'll get some more when he comes back; and be sure to come back yourself.' She gave Magnus one of her keen looks, knowing what was in the boy's mind. If he had had his way, he would have liked to stay all day on the little island with the Hermit, out of reach of the noisy invaders.

Being with Mr Skinnymalink was almost like being alone. No need for constant chatter to stave off silence. They could sit still and think their own thoughts. Or perhaps wish a wish in the Fairy Ring. Maybe the old seal would come slithering out of the sea to join them. It could be a day of pure pleasure, if only duty did not call.

'I'll have to go back,' he sighed, after he had beached the boat and hoisted out the black-faced sheep. She bleated like a lost lamb and stared around her in bewilderment. But not for long. Soon she spotted a patch of fresh grass and the next moment was chewing contentedly. The pasture here was greener and fresher than on Sula. The sheep who were rowed across enjoyed the change of diet, and were always fatter when taken home after their holiday.

'I'll come back for you as soon as the trippers are away,' Magnus promised the Hermit, as he pushed the boat off.

Mr Skinnymalink nodded and hurried away like a hunted hare to the far side of the island where he could be out of sight. Like the sheep he would soon settle down and make himself at home. There were plenty of stones to be found and polished; and as for company, he needed none. Mr Skinnymalink was self-contained.

On Sula the arrangements were well under way. The minister was pleased with himself. He had left nothing to chance. To make doubly sure he had had a word with

God about the weather; and, like a faithful servant, had been rewarded by a brilliant sun. Too brilliant, according to Gran, who took a doubtful look at the sky, shook her head and said one ominous word: 'Thunder!' But the Reverend Morrison put his trust in God, not in Gran.

Whether they liked it or not, every single soul on the island had become involved. But none as involved as Jinty Cowan. This was her great day, and she meant to make the most of it. Her knitting was discarded for the time being. She had other skills to show off to the world.

She was waiting for Magnus at the water's edge, fluffing out her feathers like Specky the hen. Certainly she was a sight for sore eyes. Magnus must be a dumb-bell not to notice. Tartan frock with touches of velvet. Lace ruffles at the neck and cuffs. White socks and patent-leather shoes. Pearl beads round her neck and bracelets dangling from her wrists. Hair in ringlets, scent behind her ears, and a dab of self-raising flour on her nose as a finishing-touch.

Magnus looked at her without noticing any of the frills and fancies. She was just Jinty Cowan, a nuisance like most lasses, but part of the familiar background of home. He would miss her if she was not there, though he wished she would learn to keep her tongue still.

Not Jinty!

'Magnus, I've got a good idea,' she greeted him as he came ashore. 'You could put on your new kilt and we'll do a dance together. Couldn't you not, Magnus?'

'No!'

'Oh well, it was just a thought.' That was one thing about Jinty, in spite of constant rebuffs she never took offence. Nor did she ever give in.

Magnus escaped from her clutches and bent down to

pat Rory who came bounding forward to meet him. The collie's master, old Cowan, was pursuing his normal tasks, ignoring the mounting excitement around him. He was busy building a dyke in the field at the back of his house.

It was a drystone dyke. Old Cowan was building it up slowly and patiently, stone upon stone, like a child playing with bricks. But this was no toy. When the work was done, it would be a permanent memorial to the old man's skill. Firmer than any fence, it would withstand wind and weather. More than that, in its ruggedness and symmetry it would be a pleasure to the eye.

Magnus went and stood beside him, appreciating the care with which the craftsman chose, discarded, and finally chipped away at the right stone to fit into his jig-saw puzzle. Old Cowan was so absorbed in his task that he might have been in another world.

Ping!

A pebble, aimed at Magnus, missed him and hit the masterbuilder on the side of his cheek.

'You wee deevil!' cried old Cowan, coming back to earth with a jolt, and rubbing his cheek angrily.

He shook his fist at the culprit. Not that the Ferret cared. Armed with his catapult, the red-headed boy had all the advantages on his side. He was perched on top of Gran's hen-house with a supply of ammunition in his pocket and the light of battle in his eye.

Magnus took up the cudgels on old Cowan's behalf.

'Come down, you, and I'll fight you,' he shouted up to the Ferret.

His spirits were rising. This was one of the things he missed most at Cronan, the rough-and-tumble of a tussle with the Ferret. There were plenty of boys at the High

School ready to put up their fists, but Magnus had not the same feeling for them. The Ferret was someone he could hate and like at the same time. The two of them could punch and kick, yet never feel any resentment at the end of the battle, however bloody. Theirs was a special relationship, difficult to define.

'Away!' scoffed the Ferret, ignoring Magnus's invitation to come down, and continuing his bombardment. He was on top, and had no intention of giving up his advantage. He was not so soft!

'Right!' said Magnus, bracing himself. 'I'll come up and get you.'

His threat was never carried out, for just then Jinty gave an excited squeal: 'They're coming!'

The excursion boat came lurching round Sula Point as if it was tipsy. It was not the sturdy old *Hebridean* but a more jaunty, gaudy-looking craft bedecked with coloured flags. *The Maid of Cronan.* She had been hired for the day, with a band playing and the decks crowded with trippers in holiday mood.

'She'll bump into the pier,' groaned old Cowan, abandoning his dyke-building to join the others on the shore. 'She's taking it too fast.'

But *The Maid* danced into harbour and drew up safely at the pier. The people on board shrieked in mock terror as the boat bumped against the landing-stage. Then they came streaming down the gangway and spilled out on to the beach as if there was not a moment to spare.

Some were carrying balloons and streamers, and sporting paper hats. 'Where are the shops?' they asked as soon as they set foot on shore. It was obvious they had come to make a day of it and were going to leave no stone unturned. They scrambled over the rocks; they climbed on to the harbour wall; they rushed up to the General Store which was sold out of sweets and soft drinks within half an hour. They chased the goat, tugged at Sheltie's tail, and poked into hen-houses and byres.

'Oh! look at the wee calfies,' they cried, gaping at Tibby's new twins and trying to feed them with lollipops and potato-crisps.

The whole island seemed to have gone haywire. Little wonder that Rory turned tail and sought refuge inside the Cowan's cottage, where he lay below the table with his head buried in his paws. Magnus, too, would have liked to escape to the sanctuary of his small bedroom, but he was pounced upon by two familiar figures. Mrs Reekie and Auntie Jessie from Cronan.

'Yoo-hoo, Magnus! We're here!'

They were both clutching shopping-bags containing all the odds and ends they might need if they had come for a month instead of a day.

Mrs Reekie beamed brightly at him and said, 'I was saying to Willy Reekie it'll be a nice wee outing and a chance to see our cousins, the Cowans. But he said he'd sooner stay at home and look after wee Ailsa, so Auntie Jessie's come to chum me. Mind your leg, Jessie. She's awful lame. And how are you, Magnus? I hear the Duke's in Sula. My word! you're fairly going up in the world. Living in the castle, no less! I used to work there in the old days, you know, before I married Willy Reekie, and so did Jessie. Didn't you, Jessie? I wonder if it's changed? Old Bella's still there, I hear. And you never come to see us at Rockview. I was saying to Willie Reekie, I wish Magnus would look in some time, wasn't I, Jessie?'

It was like a waterfall gushing at full strength. There was no stemming the flow of talk. Auntie Jessie dragged her bad leg, took a look around her and groaned, 'Deary me! I'm glad we're only here for the day. There's nothing to see. How can you stand it, Magnus? Are you not dying to get back to Cronan?'

'No,' said Magnus, 'I'm not.'

'Well, rather you than me. What is there to do?' Auntie Jessie took another look around her and made a dismal face. 'There's plenty of scenery, of course, but I'd soon get sick of it. All those seagulls! They'd get on my nerves.'

Mrs Reekie put on a more cheerful face and said, 'Och! it's not so bad today with all the trippers here, but it'll be awful lonesome once we're away. I was just saying to Willy Reekie, my! they'll be looking forward to seeing a bit of life on Sula. Oh look! There's the Cowans. Come on, Jessie; maybe we'll get a wee cup of tea.'

It was amazing how much food the trippers could consume. They had all brought supplies with them as if they were marching to war and needed iron-rations. Sandwiches, sausage-rolls, crisps, lemonade, chocolate and sweets. They flung away the wrappings with never a thought of where the litter might land. Even the smiling minister, trying to be all things to all men, clicked his false teeth and realized too late that he ought to have put up a notice: KEEP SULA TIDY.

In spite of all the supplies they had brought the tourists were soon hungry. Travel and sea-air had sharpened their appetites. Some were fortified with fly cups of tea dispensed from the cottages. They enjoyed sampling the home-made scones and pancakes which they seldom bothered to bake on the mainland. Why trouble, with so many bakers' shops within reach? It was all very well for the islanders. They had nothing else to do to pass the time!

The last man off the boat did not fit into the same pattern as the others. He seemed in no hurry to step ashore, nor was he wearing a paper hat or carrying a shopping-bag. He had been leaning over the rail gazing at everything with a critical eye, as if sizing up the island. He looked fat and prosperous, and wore towny clothes. It was easy to see, from his pale face, that most of his life had been spent indoors.

While he was strolling down the gangway he called out to Magnus, 'You! Come here! I want you!' Obviously he was used to giving orders and having them instantly obeyed. But not in Sula.

'What?' Magnus turned round and gave the man a cool look. He was no dog to be called to heel.

'Come here,' cried the man in a commanding voice. 'I want you to do something for me.'

Magnus stood his ground and made no move. The stranger gave an impatient gesture, but was forced to come after the boy. He picked his way gingerly over the pebbly beach and said sharply, 'Did you not hear me? I want you to tell me where the Duke is. I'm looking for him. Where is he?'

'He's not here,' said Magnus gruffly.

'Not here!' The man's face flushed with annoyance. 'I was told this is where I would find him. Where has he gone? I've come to Sula specially to see him.'

Magnus hesitated. He knew where the little man had gone. The Duke was on the island all right, but, like the Hermit, he was hiding from the trippers, and the boy had no intention of giving him away.

'He's somewhere,' he muttered.

'That's a stupid answer,' said the stranger crossly. 'Look here, if you don't tell me at once where he is, I'll ...'

It was the wrong tactics for him to use. Magnus began to move away. Let the man bluster as much as he liked. He was not afraid of threats.

'Wait!' cried the stranger, hurrying after him and trying to put a more friendly tone in his voice. 'I must see the Duke. It's very important. I've come a long way specially to talk to him. Not just from Cronan; all the way from London.' He thrust his hand into his pocket and brought out some money. 'Look! I'll pay you.'

Magnus shook his head. He was not to be bribed with money. 'Keep it,' he muttered and turned away.

But suddenly he paused as a thought struck him. He turned round and took a closer look at the stranger. What if the man from London had something to do with the Duke's new symphony?

He hesitated for a moment and then said: 'Okay! I'll take you to him.'

*

The excursion was in full swing. So was Miss Jinty Cowan, prima ballerina of the Scottish country dance.

Her great moment of triumph was at hand. The Reverend Alexander Morrison blew three loud blasts on his whistle to gather the scattered trippers together. They had spread-eagled all over the island. Some were tugging up bunches of heather, some gathering shells on the shore, some chasing Sheltie and the sheep. But at the shrill sound of the whistle they all came hurrying back determined not to miss anything.

'Roll up! Roll up! Come and watch the dancing,' shouted the minister, in the best fairground tradition.

'After that we'll have the tea and the sports. Come along, everybody. Roll up!'

Jinty stood poised on a little platform erected for the purpose, while old Cowan waited nearby with his concertina – the squeeze-box, he called it – at the ready. Full of confidence, she bowed to the company and raised her arms above her head.

One-two-three and she was off! Never had she danced so lightly or twirled so swiftly. The crowd cried 'Hooch!' and clapped their hands in time to the music. Cameras clicked, and Jinty's face flushed with pleasure as she heard flattering comments from all sides.

'My! isn't she a great dancer?'

'She's a wee wonder!'

'As light as a fairy.'

Jinty was in the seventh heaven. There was only one flaw. Magnus was not there to witness her triumph. He had gone off up the Heathery Hill with a stout stranger. Still, there were plenty of others crowding round to admire her performance. Even Auntie Jessie, with her bad legs, was tapping out the tune; and Mrs Reekie in a fit of high spirits linked arms with the minister and all but whirled him off his feet.

'Encore! Encore!' cried the crowd, and not in vain. Jinty could have danced for ever. Faster and faster flew her feet. She was all ringlets, ruffles, and ribbons. Her cheeks were red, her eyes sparkled. It was, without doubt, her finest hour.

Alas! how true it is that pride comes before a fall. Fate, which had been beaming so brightly on Jinty, suddenly turned sour.

It was Gran's shout of 'Tea!' that started it. When they heard the rattle of the tea-urn, the crowd melted away without even a backward glance at Jinty. It had been all very well watching the wee lassie when there was nothing better to do. But who was going to look at the Highland Fling when they might miss their tea and home-baked shortbread?

Poor Jinty! It was a hard lesson for her to learn — that human beings quickly forget, moving from one experience to the next. Off with the old love, on with the new.

Jinty's final fling ended in disaster. She had danced with such verve that the rickety platform began to creak. Suddenly it gave way. Down tumbled the ballerina in a heap of torn laces, tousled hair, scattered beads, scalding tears, and bleeding leg. The final loss of dignity came when the Ferret jeered at her, 'I can see your drawers!' and scored a direct hit with his catapult.

Jinty howled more from wounded pride than from pain. Her downfall was complete. No one took any notice of her plight. Even the District Nurse had little time or sympathy to spare. For once Mrs Gillies was fully-stretched. Over-stretched, in fact. She would have needed a dozen pairs of hands to cope with all the bites, stings, sprained ankles, and pains in the stomach, not to mention bumped heads and bleeding noses.

'Stop howling,' she said sharply to Jinty as she patched up the girl's scratched leg. 'You'll live! There! that'll have to do. I'm running out of bandages. My word! this is some day. And there's more to come.'

A lot more!

A small child scalded her arm on the tea-urn. Old Cowan's goat butted Auntie Jessie on her bad leg. A boy fell off the pier and hit his head against a rock. By the end of the day the District Nurse felt she had coped with almost everything in the Medical Dictionary. Even the minister got stung on the nose by a wasp.

'At a time like this!' scolded Mrs Gillies as she applied some soothing ointment. 'There'll be weeks when I haven't got a case of collywobbles on my hands. You might have waited, Mr Morrison.'

'The wasp wouldn't wait,' said the minister, nursing his sore nose which was now swelling to twice its size. 'Oh well, we'd better get on with the sports as soon as they've finished their teas. Where's Magnus Macduff?'

Magnus was high up on the Heathery Hill with the stout stranger from London panting at his heels like a winded dog. It was easily seen that he was not used to exercise, especially on such rough ground.

'Where on earth are you taking me?' he asked, clutching at a clump of bracken for support. 'I can't go much further. I'm dead beat.'

It occurred to Magnus that the man must, indeed, be very anxious to meet the Duke to have made such an effort. After scrambling up the hillside, his smart suit was crumpled, his shoes scuffed, and his collar and tie adrift. Altogether he looked in a sorry state.

'Wait there,' said Magnus, suddenly feeling sorry for him. 'I'll go and fetch the Duke.'

The man sank down on the heather and mopped his brow while Magnus went on round the brow of the hill till he came to the Hermit's cave. The little Duke was there, hiding like a fox in its lair, with little heaps of coloured stones around him. He was humming contentedly to himself, making music in his head.

His eyes lit up when he saw Magnus. 'Hullo boy; are you a refugee, too? Come in and join me. I can't stand these noisy trippers. Mr Skinnymalink had the right idea. Wish I had thought of going with him. Sit down, boy.'

But Magnus stayed on his feet. 'There's a man from London wanting to see you,' he told the Duke.

'What?' cried the little man in a startled voice. 'Where?'

'On the hill. He came with the excursion. Maybe it's about your music,' said Magnus, in his stilted way of speaking.

'Bless my soul!' The Duke sprang to his feet. 'You mean it's Sir Ronald Briggs? I sent him my symphony and he seemed to like it. He wrote saying he was coming to Cronan to see me. Bless my soul! Fancy following me here!'

The little man looked so excited that Magnus felt a glow of pleasure for his sake. 'That's great, Duke! Come on; the man's waiting.'

They found the stranger still sitting on the heather, looking more relaxed. He had regained his breath and his self-assured manner.

'Who's this?' he asked, looking at the shabby little Duke. His Grace was dressed in his oldest tweeds, patched at knee and elbow, with a battered deer-stalker hat stuck on his head. He could have been a tramp or a scarecrow; certainly not a blue-blooded member of the aristocracy. 'I thought you were going to fetch the Duke.'

'It's him,' said Magnus.

'Him?' The stranger took a disbelieving look at the tattered little Duke. 'Nonsense! It can't be.'

His Grace was equally taken aback. 'The wrong man! Not Sir Ronald Briggs. Never saw this one in my life before,' he said to Magnus. He turned to the stranger and said sharply, 'What is it you want with me?'

The man, realizing his mistake, had sprung to his feet. 'I'm very sorry, Your Grace,' he apologised. 'I didn't expect – er – I mean – I'm delighted to meet you. I called at the castle and was told you were here, so I caught the excursion boat.'

'What do you want?' asked the Duke impatiently. 'Come on, man. Speak up.' Shabby though he was, the Duke could be haughty enough when he liked.

'It's business, Your Grace,' said the man, pulling himself together.

'Business! Can't be bothered with it,' said the Duke, dismissing the subject.

'Wait till you hear,' protested the man, surprised at the Duke's lack of interest. He took a card from his wallet. 'There! that's my name. Ebenezer Smith of Ebenezer Smith Enterprises. I expect you have heard of us. We own holiday hotels all over the place.' He drew himself up and said proudly. 'In fact, we're the biggest concern of its kind in Britain, if not in the world. Ebenezer Smith Enterprises.'

'Never heard of them,' said the Duke, handing back the card. Enterprises of any kind were of no interest to him. 'Come on, boy,' he said to Magnus. 'We can't waste a lovely day like this.'

But Ebenezer Smith was not so easily put off. 'Wait, Your Grace, you haven't heard my proposition yet. I'll tell you what it is.' He took a deep breath to gather his forces. 'The other day in London I went to see a documentary film ... '

'What about it?' said the little Duke impatiently.

'It was called Sula, An Island Paradise,' went on

Ebenezer Smith. 'I could see at once that the place had great possibilities.'

'What for?' asked the Duke, only half-listening.

'For developing, of course,' said the man with a greedy glint in his eye. 'That's why I'm here – to make Sula into an up-to-date island paradise.'

6 Ebenezer Smith Enterprises

Ebenezer Smith, of Ebenezer Smith Enterprises, was gazing down on the island paradise spread out before him.

'Sula has everything the tourist needs for a happy holiday,' he told the Duke. 'Except, of course, proper amenities.'

'Amenities!' exploded the Duke.

'Yes, of course. Surely you can see for yourself what the place lacks.' The man from London waved his hand as if it was a magic wand and began to supply the missing amenities. 'Hotels, bathing-pools, shops, cafés, discotheques. Everything the holiday-maker demands.'

Magnus stood by, listening with horror as Ebenezer Smith went on: 'Of course, it will take a lot of money, but I'm prepared for that.' He stuck his hands in his pockets as if to finger the millions he kept there. 'It wouldn't take me long to convert this backward little island into one of the most popular holiday-resorts in Britain. I assure you, people would come flocking to it in their hundreds.'

Magnus went pale. He was used to seeing pictures in his mind's eye. Suddenly he saw the new Sula as re-made by Ebenezer Smith Enterprises. A day's excursion was bad enough. What would it be like then? The quiet cottages pulled down, skyscraper hotels towering over the harbour, The Heathery Hill dotted with painted châlets, music blaring, swarms of bathers on the beach, a night-club on Little Sula, not a corner of the island left in its natural state.

He looked at the Duke to see what effect the stranger's proposals had on him. The little man's face was red with rage. He gave Ebenezer Smith a scornful look and said sharply, 'Never heard such nonsense. Is that all? Are you finished?'

'No, I'm not!' He had not even begun. 'Can't you see what a great future there would be for the island? I could put Sula on the map and give the people a new way of life. Think what it would mean for them! Prosperity, instead of having to scratch for a bare living. Believe me, I know what I'm talking about. I've built up Ebenezer Smith Enterprises from nothing ...'

'Good-day,' said the Duke gruffly, and turned away. He had heard enough.

'Hold on!' cried Ebenezer Smith, hurrying after him. 'We haven't even begun to talk business yet. Wait a moment, Your Grace.' He thrust his hand into his pocket. 'Have a cigar.'

'No, thank you.'

Ebenezer Smith's usual methods of dealing with customers were having no effect on the eccentric little Duke. Perhaps it would be better to change his tactics and come straight to the point.

'I'll put my cards on the table, Your Grace. You must admit that, in its present state, the island has no future. Indeed, it's nothing but a liability. So what I propose is that Ebenezer Smith Enterprises should acquire it.'

'Acquire!' burst out the Duke, boiling over with rage.

'Buy it, I mean,' said the man, as if he was proposing to purchase a pair of gloves. It would be a simple enough deal for him to put through. He had done dozens of similar take-overs before.

Magnus's heart almost stopped beating when he heard the dreaded word 'buy' and saw how confident the man looked. It had never occurred to the boy that Sula was something to be bought and sold over the counter, like a bar of soap or a packet of Jinty's Dolly Mixtures. Who owned the island, anyway? Did it not belong to Gran and old Cowan and the McCallums? And to himself and the seals? Surely it was not a thing to be exchanged for money.

He glanced at the Duke and suddenly his heartbeats settled down. A load was lifted off his shoulders. Of course! Sula belonged to the little man. It was part of his heritage, like Cronan Castle and all the land surrounding it. Gran and the others rented their crofts from him, and could not hope for a better or kinder landlord. The Duke would never sell Sula to any greedy developer.

'Go away!' he wanted to shout to the man. 'Go away and leave us in peace.'

But Ebenezer Smith still had plenty to say. 'I understand the island belongs to you,' he said, giving the Duke a keen look. 'I'm sure it would be a load off your mind if you could get rid of it. I'll give you a good price.' He glanced at the Duke's threadbare garments. 'Ready cash always comes in handy.'

'Don't be ridiculous,' said the Duke angrily. 'Sula belongs to me, and I have no intention of selling it, ever!'

'Hooray!' Magnus could not stop himself from cheering. He could have clapped his hands and pushed the man down the hillside. But Ebenezer Smith had dealt with reluctant customers before, though none as odd as the little Duke. Money! That was the thing that talked. There were few who could resist it, from dust-men to dukes. Once the purse-strings were opened, it was surprising how the most reluctant could change his tune.

'Listen to me, Your Grace,' he said, as if speaking to an unreasonable child. 'I know how difficult things must be for you. I've had a look at that castle of yours and seen for myself what a state it is in. It would take a great deal of money to foot the bill for repairs. Now if you were to get rid of Sula ...'

Magnus's spirits took a downward plunge as Ebenezer Smith talked on. Everything he said was true. Magnus knew how empty the Duke's coffers were, that Cronan Castle was crumbling into decay, and that His Grace's debts were mounting up. Could the man from London, with his glib talk, persuade the penniless little Duke to change his mind?

'No! Never!' said the Duke fiercely; 'and that's the end of it.'

Magnus could have shouted 'Hooray!' again, and

louder this time. Even Ebenezer Smith saw that it would be useless to pursue the conversation. For the time being. He had sown the seeds. When the Duke had thought things over and seen the advantages, he would change his mind. Money talked.

'Very well, Your Grace. Let's leave it at that meantime; but I'll be in touch with you.' He took another card out of his wallet. 'This is my address in case you want to contact me.'

But the subject was closed as far as the Duke was concerned. He ignored both the man and the card, and said firmly to Magnus, 'Come along, boy. We've wasted enough time. You've got to help with the sports haven't you?'

'Uh-huh!' said Magnus, waking up to present realities. Even the noisy trippers would be better than Ebenezer Smith and his smooth talk. At least *they* were only taking over Sula for the day. Not for ever, as the man from London was proposing.

They left him behind without another word, and went hurrying down the hill together. 'Forget it, boy,' said the Duke, seeing that Magnus was still looking worried. 'I've dealt with fellows like that before. Nothing's going to happen.'

'Good!' said Magnus, giving him a grateful look. But the worry was still there, niggling away at the back of his mind like a headache.

Money meant as little to him as it did to the Duke. Yet he had seen during his stay at the castle how the property was falling to pieces, and knew that the bills were mounting up. It was a struggle to find enough ready-money even to pay the wages of old Bella and the gardener. The Duke's own tastes were simple enough.

Almost his only extravagance was the manuscript on which he jotted down music.

'That's it!' cried Magnus, stopping in his tracks. 'Maybe your music could make a lot of money.'

'Money!' frowned the Duke. 'Drat that fellow!' Then he gave Magnus a sideways look. 'So you think my music could make money? What about your pictures? Maybe they're worth a lot more.'

'Away!' said Magnus, looking embarrassed; but the thought had been put into his head. He would sooner keep his pictures to himself, but if it would help the Duke, he would try harder to paint something worthwhile.

*

'Magnus Macduff! Hurry up! We're ready to begin the sports.'

The Reverend Morrison's voice had a touch of irritation in it. The wasp-sting on his nose was hurting, and his brow was furrowed with worry. Though he was still trying to keep a smile on his face, it was growing more difficult every moment.

The truth was, he was becoming heartily sick of the trippers and longing to be back home in his peaceful Manse with his feet in his carpet-slippers. If only he could pronounce the benediction and get rid of them all! But there was still an hour or so before *The Maid* was due to sail.

The delights of Sula had begun to pall on the visitors, and both youngsters and grown-ups were becoming fractious. They had tried everything: wading in the sea, building sand-castles, gathering shells, scrambling up the rocks in search of birds' eggs, throwing pebbles into the water, rowing in old Cowan's boat, and riding on

Sheltie. They had eaten everything offered to them, but they were still hungry, not so much for food as for further happenings.

'My! it's been a long day,' sighed Auntie Jessie, stretching out her bad legs, as she and Mrs Reekie sat on the harbour-wall waiting like exiles to be taken home. 'The time fairly drags in a wee place like this.'

'So it does, Jessie,' agreed Mrs Reekie. 'I'll be glad to get back to Willy Reekie and wee Ailsa. There's always a bit of life in Cronan.'

'That's more than can be said of Sula,' said Auntie Jessie, gazing at a gull. 'There's nothing to see but scenery.'

'Ladies! Ladies!' called the minister with false joviality. 'Come along and watch the sports.'

'Oh well, that'll always be something,' said Mrs Reekie, brightening up. 'It'll help to pass the time. Come on, Jessie; let's see what's going on.'

The sports were taking place in old Cowan's field, a somewhat uneven racing-track, with a starting-post set up at one end and a finishing-post at the other. There were to be races for old and young, including the three-legged race, the obstacle race, the sack race, the egg-and-spoon race, as well as a sprint for boys, in which Magnus and the Ferret were to compete.

The minister urged everyone to join in, and, game to the end, took part himself in the egg-and-spoon race, finally tripping over a rough patch and falling flat on his face as he was nearing the winning-post. It did his swollen nose no good, but at least it raised a laugh from the onlookers.

The Duke and old Cowan held the tape, cheering on the runners, especially in the sprint when Magnus and the Ferret were battling for first place. Jinty, who was a non-starter in any of the events because of her sore leg, shrieked: 'Go on, Magnus! You're winning!' And, indeed, Magnus would have breasted the tape in first place if the Ferret had not deliberately tripped him up.

'Foul!' yelled the little Duke, enraged at the Ferret's lack of sportsmanship. 'Disqualify him!'

But just then something happened which brought the sports to a sudden end and sent people scuttling for shelter. The minister turned up his coat-collar and gave a resentful glance at the heavens. The Lord had let him down!

Gran had been right. The day had been too hot, the sun too bright. Now the weather broke with such fury that it seemed as if a battle was raging. Suddenly it grew as black as midnight, a flash of lightning streaked across the sky followed by a loud clap of thunder and a downpour of rain. Crash! the clouds seemed to be bumping their heads together. Flash! the darkened sky was lit up with fireworks, and the rain came teeming down in torrents, drenching everybody to the skin.

'Blast!' said the Reverend Morrison, forgetting for once his holy orders.

The excursion came to an abrupt end. There was a hasty dash towards the harbour, with everyone jostling against each other in their haste to get up the gangway and find shelter below deck. *The Maid* rocked unsteadily in the water as the Captain hastily got up steam for the return journey.

It was a sad end to such a happy outing. There were few to give the tourists a send-off, though the minister for one did his duty to the end. Throwing an old sack, left over from the sack-race, over his head, he stood on the squelching sand with the rain dripping down his face and wished the boat-load God-speed.

'O my! I'll be glad to get back to civilization,' wailed Auntie Jessie, hirpling along the wet deck and clinging to Mrs Reekie for protection. 'I'm drenched to the skin. It never rains like this in Cronan.'

'Och away, Jessie; it does sometimes,' said Mrs Reekie reasonably. 'Come away down below and we'll get ourselves dried.' She took a last look at Sula through sheets of rain and flashes of lightning. 'Poor souls!' she said, waving to the few stragglers on the shore, 'it's a shame to leave them behind. They'll fairly miss us.'

Far from missing them, the islanders were longing for the boat to leave so that, once the storm died down, they could clear up the litter left behind. Magnus more than any was wishing them gone so that he could row across to Little Sula and rescue the Hermit. How was he faring, alone in the storm? Magnus hoped he had found shelter and that he had come to no harm.

'All aboard!' called the Captain, and gave orders to pull up the gangway. But were they all on board? Where was the stranger from London, Ebenezer Smith? As *The Maid* backed out of the harbour Magnus realized he had not seen the man since he and the Duke left him on the Heathery Hill. Was he still up there? If so, someone had better tell him to hurry down.

Too late! *The Maid of Cronan* had already passed beyond the pier and was pitching and tossing across the stormy sea to the mainland.

*

A sudden silence descended on Sula. The thunder-storm had come to an end, but not the rain. It still poured down in torrents, drenching the sheep huddled against the dykes, churning the ground into mud, and sending the hens scuttling into the hen-houses for shelter. The people hurried, too, into their houses, thankful that the trippers had gone and left them in peace.

Magnus stood in Gran's doorway neither in nor out, undecided what to do first. Look for the stranger, or row across to Little Sula?

It was old Cowan who made up his mind for him. He came out from the cottage next door dressed in his oilskins.

'You'd better bring that beast of yours down the hill,' he said to Magnus. 'He seems to have got himself stuck up there.'

Sheltie! Magnus sped off through the lashing rain towards the Heathery Hill. He was wet to the skin already so it made little difference that he had not flung a sack over his shoulders. A wetting would do him no harm. He was more worried about the Shetland pony, alone and frightened by the storm.

Little rivulets were running down the hill like waterfalls. Sheltie was standing with his back hunched up staring at something lying at his feet. Magnus scurried up the hill and saw that it was Ebenezer Smith, groaning in agony.

'What's happened?' asked Magnus, bending over him.

'It's my ankle,' mumbled the man, wincing with pain. 'I can't move.'

His smart suit was sodden, his shoes covered with mud, and he looked a sorry sight lying helpless on the wet heather. In spite of his resentment against Ebenezer Smith Enterprises, Magnus felt a stab of pity for the man.

'It's all right. I'll help you to your feet,' he said,

kneeling down and trying to hoist him up. Magnus was used to handling heavy burdens, but Ebenezer Smith – fat and flabby as he was – was a dead weight, more awkward to handle than a load of peat or any of Gran's sheep.

'It's no use,' said the man, sinking back. Then suddenly he made an effort to ease himself up and muttered, 'Must catch the boat.'

'It's away,' said Magnus.

Ebenezer Smith sank back in despair. 'When is the next one?' he asked anxiously.

'There's not another till the *Hebridean* comes next week,' Magnus told him.

'What?' For a moment the man forgot his pain and sat bolt upright. 'But I must get back to London. I have important business to do.' But even business, important or otherwise, had no power over the man's weakness. Suddenly he fell back looking so pale that Magnus thought he had fainted.

'I'll go and get help,' he said, and scrambled to his feet. 'Come on, Sheltie.'

Magnus led the pony down to the foot of the hill and then jumped on his back. The rain suddenly stopped as if a tap had been turned off. A coloured arc appeared in the sky, and the sun beamed out as brightly as before.

The wet hens emerged, shaking out their feathers; the sheep moved away from their shelters; the people came out of their cottages like puppets appearing from their weather-houses, and the whole island burst into life once more.

Magnus made straight for old Cowan who was about to resume his work on the dyke, and told his tale.

'Mercy on us!' cried the old man, but, without wasting

time with needless questions, he said, 'You'd better fetch Mrs Gillies and get help to carry him down. I'll look for a plank of wood to use as a stretcher.'

When he heard the news, the little Duke was none too pleased to know that Ebenezer Smith was still on the island.

'That fellow!' he exploded. 'I thought we'd got rid of him.' His face lengthened as he realized the man would have to stay in Sula till the *Hebridean* was due. Then, humanity overcame his other feelings and he said briskly, 'Come on, boy. I'll lend a hand to carry him down.'

'Where'll we take him?' asked the District Nurse, as the little group of volunteers wound their way down the hill bearing their burden on the improvised stretcher. Mrs Gillies had already examined her patient and discovered that the ankle was badly sprained. It would mend easily enough, but the man was suffering from exposure following the drenching rain, and in the District Nurse's opinion, was already in poor shape from an overdose of soft living.

There was no room to spare in the schoolhouse or in any of the cottages, so the minister gave a self-righteous sigh and said, 'I suppose he had better come to the Manse.' It had been a day of tribulation as well as triumph for him. His wasp-sting was hurting and he was still longing for his carpet-slippers. 'Though, mind you,' he warned, 'the spare bed'll be damp. It hasn't been slept in for years.'

'Mrs Morrison can put a couple of pigs in it,' said the District Nurse sharply, referring to the stone hot-water-bottles with which the islanders heated their beds in wintry weather. 'You'd better go on ahead, Mr Morrison, and warn your wife.'

It was not only the minister who was at the end of his tether. After such a day, Florence Nightingale's lamp was burning very low.

The minister's wife, a pale echo of her husband, grew even paler when he broke the news to her; but she was not named Martha for nothing. By the time the uninvited guest arrived, she had boiled the kettle, spread clean sheets on the bed, and inserted the hot pigs.

Ebenezer Smith lay moaning to himself in the spare room, not so much from pain as from frustration. He was thinking of his crowded desk in his busy London office, and of all the deals awaiting his decisions. And here he was, trapped in a poky little bedroom at the back of beyond, with peony-roses on the wallpaper and a wet seagull sitting on the window-sill.

'Where's that boy?' he called out to Mrs Morrison, who was hovering at the door with a tray of tea and toast.

'Which boy?' she asked nervously, kicking the door open with her foot.

'I don't know which boy,' said the man irritably. 'The one who found me on the hill.'

'Oh! Magnus Macduff,' said Mrs Morrison, setting down the tray. 'Sit up and have your tea, Mr Smith; and here's a pill the District Nurse says you're to swallow.'

'Fetch that boy,' he said sharply. 'I want him to send some telephone messages for me.' Mrs Morrison looked the kind of person he could order about; and, indeed, she went meekly away to do his bidding. It was no use asking her husband. The minister was already sitting by the fire in his slippers, with a DO NOT DISTURB look on his face.

Magnus, as it happened, was within hailing distance but had better things to do than obey Ebenezer Smith's commands. He shook his head at Mrs Morrison and said, 'I'm not coming. I'm away across to Little Sula to fetch Mr Skinnymalink. I'll maybe come when I get back.'

Maybe yes, and maybe no!

'All right, Magnus,' sighed Mrs Morrison and turned away, knowing there was no more to be said. She trailed upstairs and told her guest, 'He's busy. He can't come just now. You'd better drink up your tea while it's hot.'

Mr Ebenezer Smith sat up in bed wearing a pair of the minister's patched pyjamas and one of Mrs Morrison's knitted shawls round his shoulders. A feeling of desolation came over him as he hit his foot against one of the stone bottles and realized that, for the first time in his life he was powerless, with no office staff at his command and only the minister's wife as a slave. What would happen to Ebenezer Smith Enterprises without his hand on the tiller?

He stared at a text hanging opposite him on the rosy wallpaper. COUNT YOUR BLESSINGS. He sneezed, and some of his tea slopped over into his saucer. Then suddenly a crafty glint came into his eye. Perhaps his accident would prove to be a blessing in disguise. A few days on the island would give him the opportunity to break down the little Duke's resistance.

'That's right,' he told himself, tucking the shawl more firmly round his shoulders. 'Count your blessings! I'll have Sula all tied up before I leave.'

7 Surprises

'Magnus! Wait till you hear!'

Jinty Cowan had a million things to tell Magnus when he came rowing back from Little Sula. She was so eager that she almost ran straight into the water to meet him.

Jinty was still wearing her tattered finery and the bandage on her leg; but for once she had other things to think about than her own appearance. In Magnus's absence she had been summoned to the Manse to act as runner for the stranger from London.

'Mr Smith, that's his name. Mr Ebenezer Smith. Look how much money he's given me. He's a millionaire. He's been giving me messages for his London office. We've to send them through the telephone, and I'm to take back the answers. Fancy having a millionaire in

Sula! Isn't it exciting, Magnus?'

Magnus pushed past her with a stricken look on his face. He hardly saw her or heard what she was saying. He could only think of one thing. Where was Mr Skinnymalink?

He had been forced to come back alone from Little Sula after a frenzied search all over the small island.

At first he had wondered if the Hermit was hiding from him, but Mr Skinnymalink was not likely to play such childish pranks. Then a fearsome thought came into the boy's head. What if Mr Skinnymalink had been struck by lightning during the storm? Or could he have fallen into the sea and been drowned?

'Mr Skinnymalink! Mr Skinnymalink!' he called out, with rising panic in his voice.

No reply, except for the bleating of the black-faced sheep and the cry of the gulls. Magnus went white with fear. His heart was thumping with terror as he ran here and there, searching in every nook and cranny. There was only one small cave, but it was empty save for a small heap of coloured stones. The Hermit had been here, but where was he now?

The boy went and stood desolately in the Fairy Ring taking a last look around the little island. Then he shut his eyes tightly. If ever he needed a wish it was now. 'Please!' he pleaded, 'let me find Mr Skinnymalink, safe and alive.' But when he opened his eyes he could see nothing but a sheep staring up at him.

What was he to do? There was no use staying here. He had better row back and raise the alarm. Gran would know what must be done.

As he sailed over the choppy sea back to Sula he scanned the water, afraid that he might see a floating body. A dark shape, tossed by the waves, came bumping against the boat, but it was only Old Whiskers.

When he reached the shore Magnus beached the boat, ran past Jinty Cowan, and rushed into Gran's cottage.

'Gran! Gran!' he called out in a trembling voice. 'I can't find Mr Skinnymalink. He's not there!'

Specky the hen fluttered out of his way as the boy skidded to a stop and stood staring at a figure seated at the kitchen table, supping a bowl of broth. It was the Hermit with a blanket round his shoulders and his wet jacket steaming on the clothes-horse in front of the fire. The *winter-dyke*, Gran called it.

Magnus gaped at him like a gull. 'Mr Skinnymalink!' he gasped out. 'How on earth did you get here?'

'I went and fetched him, of course,' said Gran sharply. 'I didn't want him to catch his death of cold.'

Magnus was so relieved to see the Hermit alive and well that he could find no words to express his feelings, beyond: 'Are you all right, Mr Skinnymalink?'

The Hermit looked up at him and nodded. He was none the worse, especially with Gran's good broth inside him. She refilled his bowl and ladled out a helping for Magnus.

'There!' she said, pushing a platter full of oatcakes towards him. 'Eat! Then you can go and help to tidy the mess the trippers have left.' She shot a quick glance at the boy and asked, 'What about that man from London? The one who's staying at the Manse.'

Magnus looked uneasy. 'He came to see the Duke,' he told her. 'He wants to buy Sula.'

Gran let out a short sharp exclamation and rattled the ladle into the soup-pot. 'He's wasting his time. The Duke would never sell.'

'No,' said Magnus; but the niggling fear came back into his mind. Even to speak about it made him feel troubled; but Gran had no more to say on the subject. Instead, she turned her attention to the Hermit. Shifting his coat on the winter-dyke nearer to the fire, she said, 'It'll soon be dry. You'd better go and sleep in the school-house tonight.'

Mr Skinnymalink nodded. When Gran ordered him to do anything he always obeyed, and, indeed, with the warmth and the food he was half-asleep already.

Magnus was hastily supping his broth and eating his oatcake. 'I'll take you there, Mr Skinnymalink,' he offered. He had to help the Hermit to his feet and button him into his coat like a child. Then, holding him by the arm, Magnus led him away towards the schoolhouse.

Jinty sped past them with an important look on her face. 'Another message! For Mr Ebenezer Smith,' she cried, waving a piece of paper in her hand. 'It came through the telephone. I'm awful busy!'

As she hurried away on her mission, the uneasy feeling came back to disturb Magnus. What was Mr Smith plotting as he lay in the Manse bedroom? He hoped it had nothing to do with buying the island. But when he saw the Duke waiting at the schoolhouse door, Magnus's heart lightened. The shabby little man was whistling away to himself as he scanned the evening sky with a blissful look on his face.

'Hullo, boy,' he called out cheerfully. 'Isn't it peaceful? Thank goodness the trippers are gone. It'll be even better when we get rid of that London fellow. I'll be glad to see the back of him.'

'Me, too,' said Magnus, breathing more easily.

The Duke grasped the Hermit by the arm and said,

'Come along, Mr Skinnymalink. You look all in. No games for us tonight. Straight to bed!'

As he led the Hermit away, the schoolmaster came to the door. 'Hullo, Magnus,' he said. 'I've been working on my book. What about you? Have you done any drawings?'

'M-m!' said Magnus cautiously.

'Perhaps you'll let me have a look at them some time,' ventured Andrew Murray.

'I might,' said Magnus, and turned away before he was forced to commit himself.

*

Next morning a stealthy figure could be seen lurking behind the rockery in the Manse garden. The Ferret, bent on mischief as usual.

Though the Reverend Morrison worked hard in his garden he had little enough to show for his pains. It was not easy to cultivate flowers in such poor soil. A few peony-roses struggled for existence alongside a clump of candytuft, a sprig of southernwood and a bush of flowering-currant. There were some rows of potatoes and cabbages and a straggle of scraggy berry-bushes. But the main feature was the rockery which he and his wife had built up over the years.

Its foundation was made up of old tubs, pails, stones, and shells, all carefully covered with soil in which sea-pinks, primulas, forget-me-nots, and small flowering bushes were striving to make a brave show. The minister tended it each day with great care, poking at it here and there with a trowel, examining any new bloom and extracting every weed. It was his pride and joy.

Today it was looking its best in the morning sunshine. The splash of colour had attracted some bright butterflies; and a bevy of bees buzzed around, making a pleasant humming sound. It was a sound seldom heard by Ebenezer Smith who was sitting in an old deck-chair under the stunted rowan tree, with his foot stretched out on a small stool.

'You can get up if you like and sit in the garden,' the District Nurse had told him. 'The air'll do you good, Mr Smith. You're looking very peely-wally.'

'Very what?' asked Ebenezer Smith in a startled voice.

'Peely-wally,' repeated Mrs Gillies firmly. 'Sickly-looking. You should get more fresh air.'

'Nonsense! I'm far too busy,' he muttered impatiently.

'Rubbish!' A millionaire he might be, but Mrs Gillies was in no way intimidated by him. Mr Ebenezer Smith was only another patient. 'You can always find time. After all, nobody's too busy to die.'

As he sat under the rowan tree, her words rang in his ears like a warning bell. 'Nobody's too busy to die.' Watching the bright butterflies fluttering over the flowers in the rockery, he began to wonder if he had been too busy to live.

Just then two things happened to divert his thoughts from himself. The minister came out with his watering-can, and a pebble from the Ferret's catapault came whizzing through the air. He had been aiming at a bee winging its way across the garden, but the pebble narrowly missed the minister's nose instead.

It was a tender enough spot already; and His Reverence let out an angry exclamation. 'You young devil! Wait till I get hold of you. I'll box your ears.'

The Ferret had no intention of waiting. He jumped to his feet to make a hasty get-away, but in his hurry he overbalanced and toppled forward into the rockery.

The foundations, loosened by yesterday's rain-storm, gave way under the Ferret's weight. Down tumbled every stone, tub, pail, shell, and plant, with the boy lying sprawling in the ruins and the minister watching all his patient work disintegrate before his eyes.

'Damnation!' he shouted out, clutching his brow in despair. Then he doubled his fists and took a dive forward to get his revenge on the Ferret. *Suffer the little children.*

The Ferret was too quick for him. He sprang to his feet, covered with soil, fronds of fern and sprigs of forget-me-nots, leapt over the wreckage and took to his heels at lightning speed.

His catapult had landed at the feet of Ebenezer Smith who had watched the drama with great interest. He picked it up and handed it to the enraged minister who shoved it in his pocket and cried, 'The young devil! I'll make him suffer for this. Look at the mess! It took years to build that rockery. Years! And look at it now!'

It was too much to bear, even for a man of God. His face was red with rage and he kicked out at the watering-can to relieve his feelings. He would sooner have been kicking the Ferret, but he was already speeding away towards the Heathery Hill where he meant to hide till the storm had died down.

Justice, however, was overtaking him in the shape of a boy on a white pony. Magnus had been riding like a rancher round old Cowan's field, helping him to round up his sheep, when he heard the commotion and spurred his steed towards the Manse garden. He could see as he passed by what had happened, and though he had a fellow-feeling for the Ferret, he knew that the boy must be brought to justice.

'Come on, Sheltie.' He kicked the pony with his bare heels and galloped after the runaway. The Ferret had no choice. Before long he was rounded up like one of the sheep.

'You'd better go back,' said Magnus in a reasonable tone. 'You can build up the rockery.'

'Not me!' said the Ferret defiantly. He wiped some of the soil from his grazed knees and grunted, 'The minister'll murder me.'

Normally Magnus would have jeered 'Fearty!' at him. But he somehow sensed that this would be the wrong approach. Instead he jumped off the pony's back and said, 'Come on! I'll give you a hand.'

Without waiting, he turned and set off towards the Manse with the pony trotting by his side. He did not look round to see if the Ferret was following, but he guessed he would come. For one thing, he would want to get his catapult back.

There was no one in the garden except Ebenezer Smith still sitting in the deck-chair under the rowan tree. The minister had gone inside to cool his rage in his study. Magnus ignored the man from London, and surveyed the wreckage for a moment before setting to work to rebuild the rockery.

It was difficult to know where to start, but he did his best to gather up the scattered stones, shells, pails and tubs, and to fit the plants and shrubs back into place. Soon he was helped by another pair of hands. The Ferret, looking over his shoulder now and again to see if the minister was coming, began to do his share of fetching and carrying.

The little Duke, passing by, peered over the hedge and asked, 'What's going on, boy?'

'Nothing,' said Magnus briefly. 'The rockery fell down.' He did not say how, nor did the Duke ask any more questions. Instead, he jumped over the hedge to join them. He almost jumped back again when he saw who was sitting under the rowan tree.

'Him!' he hissed to Magnus, as he stooped down to pick up a handful of broken sea-shells.

'Never heed him,' said Magnus; but he was conscious of Mr Ebenezer Smith sitting up and taking more interest in the scene now that the Duke had arrived. Presently he could hear him clearing his throat and calling: 'Could I have a word with you, Your Grace?'

'No!' said the Duke sharply, without turning round.

Ebenezer Smith was not so easily put off. 'I was wondering,' he called out, 'if you had reconsidered ... '

'No!' said the Duke, even more sharply. He lifted up a lump of rock as if he meant to fling it at the man. Instead, he fitted it firmly into the rockery, and looked so forbidding that even Ebenezer Smith thought it better not to try again. He eased his foot on the stool in front of him, gave a self-pitying sigh and settled back in his chair. It was the first time in his life he had sat still for so long without promoting any of his business interests. All he could do was watch the activity at the rockery and listen to the call of the sea-birds circling overhead.

Magnus had found an old besom and was sweeping up the loose soil from the grass when the minister came out. His Reverence, having worked himself into a calmer frame of mind, was more able to face adversity, and ready to tackle the task of rebuilding his ruined rockery. When he saw that the work was already done, a beaming smile flashed across his face and he cried out, 'Well done!' He was even ready to forgive the Ferret, but the red-headed boy had already taken to his heels without waiting to ask for his catapult.

'I'm afraid it's a little lopsided,' said the Duke, giving a few final pats to a clump of sea-pinks as he tried to settle them back into the soil.

'Never mind; I can soon put things right. After all, accidents will happen,' said the minister, still in a forgiving mood. 'You'll stay and have some coffee, Your Grace?'

'No, I won't,' said His Grace in his uncompromising way, to the disappointment of Ebenezer Smith who had sat up ready to join in the conversation. As the Duke turned away, young Jinty Cowan came whizzing through the gate.

'Another message from London!' she called out, full of importance. 'It's not for you this time, Mr Smith. It's for the Duke.' She bobbed a little curtsey to His Grace and held out a telegram, which he thrust into his pocket.

'Come on, boy,' he said to Magnus. 'Are you finished?'

'Uh-huh!' said Magnus, wiping his hands. Then he hesitated. There was one more job he must do. He drew a deep breath and went up to the minister. 'Could I have the Ferret's catapult back?' As the minister drew his brows together in a frown, Magnus added, 'Please!' an unusual word for him, but he felt that the occasion warranted it.

'Oh well,' said the Reverend Morrison, relenting. He thrust his hand into his pocket and brought out the catapult. 'Forgive and forget! But tell that laddie to keep well out of my way for a day or two.'

'Yes, sir,' said Magnus, transferring the catapult to his own pocket before speeding away after the Duke.

Jinty hovered like one of the butterflies at the Manse

gate, hoping she might be invited to join them, or that the minister would say, 'Don't go away, Jinty. Come in and give us your crack.' But nobody took any notice of her. It was hard lines. She gave a sigh and then consoled herself with the thought of her secret plan.

'Wait till I get to the High School at Cronan. Nothing'll stop me then.'

*

Magnus and the Duke were sitting side-by-side on the harbour wall. In the distance they could see Tair trundling the pram, taking the twins out for their first airing since their illness. Avizandum had fled from his pocket in a huff. Tair was too absorbed with his young charges to pay attention to him. 'Coo-coo! Puff-puff! Shoo-shoo!' No wonder Avizandum was fed up.

Suddenly the Duke turned to Magnus and said, 'I want to have a serious talk with you, boy.'

Magnus looked at the Duke in alarm. What was he going to tell him? That he had changed his mind about selling Sula?

'It's about Andrew Murray,' said the Duke in a solemn tone. 'I'm worried about him.'

For a moment Magnus was so relieved that he hardly heard what the little Duke was saying about the schoolmaster. Why should anyone be worried about him?

'He seems to be very listless,' the Duke said. 'Just sitting about as if he had lost interest in everything. Of course, it takes years to recover from an illness like his. Years and years.'

Magnus vaguely knew that the reason why the young teacher had come to live in Sula was to regain his health after an attack of polio. The quiet life and the good air seemed to suit him; and though at first he had been regarded as an incomer, he was now accepted as a member of the community.

'He needs taking out of himself,' said the Duke. He swiped at a bee buzzing round his head, and then took a quick look at Magnus. 'You could maybe help him, boy.'

'Me?' said Magnus, startled.

'That book of his; you know, the one about Sula. He seemed keen enough about it for a time, but now he's lost interest in it. He says it'll be no use without the right pictures.' The Duke gave Magnus another quick look. 'I think he was hoping you might illustrate it for him. Would you not try, boy?'

Magnus kicked his bare heels. There was a guilty feeling at his heart. He had always shied away from any approach of friendship from the schoolmaster. Yet it was Andrew Murray who had encouraged him more than anyone else to use his talent for drawing. Often the boy had wanted to say thank you to him, but always he feared he might be trapped into an intimacy from which he could not escape.

Now he had a chance to settle his debt. 'I've done some drawings,' he confided to the Duke.

'You have! Well done, boy!' cried the little man, jumping down from the wall. 'Come on; let me see them, then I'll show them to Andrew. It's just what he needs, to spur him on.'

There was no one in Gran's kitchen except Specky the hen pecking hopefully on the floor for a few crumbs. The Duke looked at the picture on the wall, but said nothing. That was one of the things Magnus liked best about the strange little man, his ability to hold his tongue when words should not be spoken.

Magnus led the way up the steep stairs to his bedroom, and picked up his drawing-book. The Duke perched himself on the bed and leafed his way through the pages.

'By jove, boy,' he cried, 'you've got it!'

The whole of Sula was there in the book. Not only the birds, the seals, the scenery, the new-born calves, the Fairy Ring. People, too: Gran, the Ferret, the McCallum twins, and a lean scarecrow of a figure, the Hermit, sitting polishing away at his stones.

'They're perfect!' cried the Duke, his face beaming with pleasure. 'Let me take them to show Andrew. He'll be thrilled when he sees them.' He paused and looked questioningly at the boy. 'Or maybe you'd like to come and show them to him yourself.'

'No,' said Magnus, hanging back. He would let the Duke take the pictures, but he was wary of becoming too involved with the schoolmaster. He would pay his debt by letting the man have the drawings, but that was as far as he would go.

A handful of pebbles came rattling against the window-pane.

'What's that?' asked the Duke.

Magnus knew the signal. 'It's the Ferret,' he said, and went to push up the window. 'What are you wanting?' he shouted, hanging out his head.

'I want my catapult,' mumbled the Ferret, looking up.

Without it, he was only half alive. It was as constant a companion to him as Avizandum was to Tair. The Ferret knew it was in Magnus's pocket. Little Miss Know-All had told him about the minister handing it over.

Magnus knew that he was one up on the Ferret. He could have made him beg for the catapult. Or he could have suggested fighting for it. There were all kinds of bargains he could have made before giving it up. It was a great feeling of power – till he saw the Ferret's dejected look.

'There!' he said, flinging the catapult down. 'Take it.' But he could not resist adding a jibe. 'Look out, or I'll come down and thump your nose.'

The Ferret caught the catapult, grinned up at him and stuck out his tongue, before running away, feeling whole and alive again.

The incident had reminded the Duke that there was something in his own pocket. The telegram Jinty had given him. He was not in the least anxious to find out its contents. Telegrams meant trouble. Or business. They were all very well for the likes of Mr Ebenezer Smith and his Enterprises; but the Duke could keep one in his pocket for weeks without troubling to open it.

He took it out, fingered it, and then stuffed it back. The day was too sunny to bother himself with bad news.

'I'm off!' he said, picking up the drawings to take to the schoolteacher. 'What are you going to do, Magnus?'

'Me?' said Magnus, turning back from the window. There were a hundred things he could do. Row across to Little Sula. Ride on Sheltie's back. Go and visit the Hermit. Lie on a rock beside Old Whiskers. Go for a swim in the sea.

There was no need for him to make up his mind. Gran was calling to him from below.

'Mag-nus! Are you there? Have you fed the cow? Mag-nus! Come and bring in the peat.'

'Yes, Gran; I'm coming.'

8 A Strange Day

It all began as a quiet enough day in Sula, the day that was to be the strangest in Magnus's life.

'Mercy me! it looks almost life-like,' cried Mrs Gillies, jumping off her her bicycle in surprise. She propped the bicycle against the dyke and stared at an object set up in the midst of old Cowan's potato-patch. 'It's given me quite a turn. I could have sworn it was human. It's some scarecrow, that!'

Old Cowan was half-proud half-ashamed of his new scarecrow. A *tattie-bogle*, he called it. The old one had fallen to pieces, and he had meant to replace it with a new one, as plain and simple as the other. Anything to scare away the thieving crows. But he had not reckoned with so many volunteer assistants.

He had begun with the body, using an old besom-shank for the purpose, and was about to fix on a wooden head when the children came crowding round him, willing to help. Too willing. Especially Jinty who had ideas about how the tattie-bogle should be dressed.

'Wait! I'll find an old skirt,' she said, and went scurrying away to rummage in her mother's wardrobe. The others, too, ran backwards and forwards, fetching cast-off garments. Before long the scarecrow was arrayed in a complete outfit of discarded finery, including a patched tartan jacket, a long skirt frayed round the edges, a straw hat with faded flowers, and a feather boa.

'She's got everything but a face,' said Jinty. 'Magnus, can't you not ... ?'

But Magnus, carried away like the others, had already run inside to fetch his paint-box.

'My goodness! she's a work of art,' cried old Cowan as he watched the boy giving the newly born scarecrow a pair of blue eyes, arched eyebrows, a neat little nose, a rosy mouth, and blushing cheeks. 'We'll need to christen her.'

'Flora Macdonald!' said Jinty promptly. 'We could call the next one Bonnie Prince Charlie.' She gave a romantic look at the young artist and said, 'You're awful clever, Magnus.'

'Away!' said Magnus, feeling a little ashamed of having wasted his good paints on a mere tattie-bogle. He hurried away with his paint-box into Gran's cottage while old Cowan gingerly lifted Flora Macdonald and set her down amongst the potatoes.

'Don't shoogle her,' said Jinty anxiously. 'Her hat'll fall off. D'you think I should find an old umbrella to put over her head in case she gets wet?'

'Don't be daft,' grunted old Cowan. 'You've gone far enough. Away you go, the lot of you.'

It was at this point that the District Nurse arrived on the scene, astonished to see what appeared to be a newcomer to the island standing upright in the field.

'I don't know if she'll frighten the crows but she certainly gave me a turn.' Mrs Gillies was already speaking of Flora Macdonald as if she was real. 'You wait till the minister sees her. He'll be raising his hat!'

Old Cowan turned his back on the scarecrow and changed the subject by asking, 'How's that London chap? Is he better?'

'Him!' said Mrs Gillies impatiently. 'He's got business on the brain. Business! I've told him he'd be healthier doing a real job with his hands.' She took another look at Flora Macdonald before remounting her bicycle. 'Come on; get a move on,' she told herself. 'You'll never get anywhere if you stay blethering here.' And away she went, tinkling her bell to scatter the cocks and hens out of her path.

The District Nurse's advice had not been entirely wasted on Ebenezer Smith who for once was using his hands instead of puzzling his brains about how to make more money. He was pottering in the Manse garden, patching up the rockery, pulling out weeds, and tidying the border.

Already his face looked less pallid. Less *peely-wally*, Mrs Gillies would have called it. There was more colour in his cheeks, his eyes looked brighter, and he seemed less restless and arrogant. The fresh air of Sula and the peaceful surroundings were working wonders.

A new feeling of contentment had come over him. Even the link that bound him to his desk in London seemed less important. He was sending and receiving fewer messages, and had almost forgotten the reason for his visit to Sula. Almost, but not quite.

Suddenly he laid down his trowel and decided to make one more effort to see the Duke. The old urge was still there, though it was less strong. Ebenezer Smith was not going to give in without one final try.

He had to hobble along the rough road with the aid of the minister's walking-stick. His progress was slow, giving him time to look round at the property he had come to acquire. Sula! With the business side of his brain he could see it humming with activity, with holiday-makers swarming off the boats in their hundreds. He might even fly them in by air if he could build a landing-strip somewhere on the island. The more tourists, the more money for Ebenezer Smith Enterprises.

He stopped to lean against old Cowan's stone dyke and caught sight of Flora Macdonald standing in the potato-patch. The stillness of the scarecrow and the calmness of the island scene drove away his unquiet thoughts and brought back to his mind the District Nurse's warning words. Would it not be better to forget about money, and leave the simple people of Sula to enjoy their peaceful lives in their own way?

Jinty Cowan came skipping towards him with the newly knitted scarf slung round her neck. She was waiting for an opportunity to present it to Magnus, but in the meantime she wanted all and sundry to admire her handiwork. There were a few dropped stitches here and there, but Jinty could close her eyes to such flaws.

'Look, Mr Smith,' she cried, untwining the scarf from her neck. 'I knitted this myself. For Magnus.'

'Where is he?' asked Ebenezer Smith, more interested

in the boy than the scarf, knowing that in Magnus he had a link with the Duke. If he could get the boy on his side it would be easier to break down the barriers with His Grace. That is, if he decided to pursue his plan of buying Sula.

'Magnus?' Jinty swivelled round on her heels and pointed towards the rocks. 'He's there, in the sea with the seals.' She shot a warning glance at Ebenezer Smith and said, 'You'd better not go near him, Mr Smith.'

But at least he could look, and what he saw made him catch his breath at the beauty of it. Never before had he seen such an unusual sight, a boy swimming amongst the seals as if he was one of their own kind. They were all turning and twisting in the water, rubbing their bodies against each other, and frisking together like playful children.

It was a picture Ebenezer Smith would never forget, long after he was back in the turmoil of his busy London office. The memory of it would act as a brake to slow him down and make him realize that there were better things to be seen than his bank-book.

'Any more messages, Mr Smith?' asked Jinty, breaking into his reverie.

'Messages?' Ebenezer Smith shook his head. He was in no mood for messages. All the same, now that he had come so far, he might as well continue his journey to the schoolhouse.

He left Jinty and went hobbling away to knock at Andrew Murray's door. From inside he could hear the strains of music, rippling tunes which seemed to be speaking of the sea splashing in to the shore, of the boy swimming with the seals, of the quiet islanders going about their daily tasks, even of the scarecrow standing in the field. He listened for a long time, not wanting to break the spell. But presently the teacher's little dog, Trix, began to bark, sensing the presence of a stranger on the doorstep, and the music stopped abruptly.

It was the Duke himself who came to the door with his fiddle tucked under his arm, looking none too pleased when he saw who was standing there. 'What do you want?' he asked, shortly.

'I want,' began Ebenezer Smith, and then stopped, not knowing what he wanted. To buy Sula? To tell His Grace how much he had enjoyed his music? To express his feelings about Magnus and the seals? To make a friend instead of a foe of the fiery little Duke?

'Come in,' called a voice, more hospitable than the Duke's. The schoolmaster, with Magnus's drawings laid out on the table, looked up and said in a friendly voice, 'You'd better come and sit down. How's the sore foot?'

'Better,' said Ebenezer Smith, limping in and settling himself down on a chair by the table. He glanced at the drawings and opened his eyes wide when he saw how perfect they were. 'Are these done by a local artist?' he asked, though he could hardly believe that anyone in Sula was capable of such fine work.

It was to be a day of surprises for him. First, that the shabby little Duke was such an accomplished musician; and now that the artist who could draw such brilliant pictures was living on the island.

'It's Magnus Macduff,' said the schoolmaster, spreading out the pictures so that his visitor could see them better.

'That boy!' cried Ebenezer Smith. 'Good gracious, he's a genius!' He examined the pictures one after another, and asked, 'What are you going to do with them?'

'I'm writing a book,' said the schoolmaster, 'and I'm hoping to use Magnus's pictures to illustrate it.'

Once more Ebenezer Smith opened his eyes wide with surprise. So much talent in Sula! Where else could he find a writer, a musician, and an artist in such a small community? What had he to offer them? Prosperity that they did not want? Gaudy shops and cafés, an easier way of life with more money in their pockets and more artificial goods to buy? Or would they not be better off if he left them to rule their own lives, as they had done in the past?

Now that he was here he might as well make one last effort to pursue his own interests. He looked up at the Duke, absorbed in tuning his fiddle-strings.

'About that proposition, Your Grace,' he began.

'The subject's closed,' said the Duke, twanging the fiddle-strings angrily. Would the fellow never learn to take No for an answer?

At that moment Jinty Cowan came hurtling through the door with her skipping-rope over her arm and Magnus's scarf dangling from her neck.

''Scuse me, but you're wanted on the tellyphone,' she said breathlessly. 'It's very urgent. From London. They're hanging on.'

'They'll have to wait,' said Ebenezer Smith, picking up the minister's walking-stick. 'I can't walk fast.'

'Oh, it's not for you, Mr Smith,' Jinty told him. She bobbed one of her little curtsies to the Duke. 'It's for you, Your Grace.'

'Me? I don't want any telephone calls. Tell them to go away.'

'Oh, but it's very important, Your Grace,' said Jinty with another little bob. 'The man said it was about the telegram.'

'What telegram?' began the Duke, then remembered it was still in his pocket unopened. He laid down his fiddle, extracted the crumpled telegram and tore open the envelope.

As he read the message, the little man's face changed colour. First it went white, then a rosy glow seemed to light him up from within. He looked round at the others in a daze, not seeing them, and made straight for the door on his way to the Post Office.

'I wonder what's up?' said Jinty, trying to make up her mind to run after him and hover near the telephone. If there was any drama going, it would be a pity to miss it. On the other hand, this might be a golden opportunity to speak to the schoolmaster about her own affairs. Her plan to go to the Girls' High School at Cronan. It was becoming more and more difficult to keep the secret to herself. Maybe she should tell Mr Murray and ask his advice.

'Please, sir,' she began, putting up her hand as if she was in the classroom. 'I've got something to ask you.'

'Not now, Jinty,' said Andrew Murray impatiently. He saw enough of Little Miss Know-All in the schoolroom. During the holidays he tried to avoid her as much as possible.

'Oh well,' sighed Jinty, defeated once more. 'I'll away!' She could always go back home and find out about the Duke's telephone call.

The Ferret was sitting on the dyke pinging away at Flora Macdonald with his catapult. It was great to have found a new target, especially one who could not hit back.

'Stop it, you!' cried Jinty 'You'll knock off her hat.'

'I'll knock off your head,' retaliated the Ferret, turning his attention to Jinty instead. At least, *she* would squeal, which was more than he could expect from the scarecrow.

Jinty scuttled past him in an effort to get out of his range, but she was not quick enough. She let out a scream as she felt a stinging blow on her bare leg; and the Ferret, satisfied, gave a chuckle and returned to his ploy of peppering away at the scarecrow.

Jinty ran slap-bang into the Duke as he emerged from the Post Office, having completed his call. 'Oh, beg pardon, Your Grace,' she cried, pulling herself back, but he took no notice of her except to ask in an excited voice, 'Where's Magnus?' The rosy glow was still on his face. Jinty could see that he had some great piece of news to tell; but, alas! not to her.

'Magnus? Don't know, Your Grace. He was in the sea with the seals ...'

The little man was off like a shot. At any other time he would not have disturbed the boy when he was with Old Whiskers and the other seals. But this was different. He must see him at once and tell him the great news.

'Hullo, boy,' he shouted as he ran across the shingly beach. 'Ahoy there! Where are you, Magnus?'

There was no response. The Duke could see the young seals sporting in the water, but Old Whiskers was missing and so was the boy.

'He must have come out of the sea and gone home,' thought the little man, turning on his tracks. He hurried up to the cottages and rapped on Gran's door.

The old woman was down on her knees scrubbing the kitchen floor which seemed spotless enough already.

Specky had flown up on to the table to be out of the way, and was making clucking sounds to herself as if about to lay an egg.

'He's not here,' said Gran, shaking the soapy water from her scrubbing-brush. 'It's time he was back. I'm needing him to do some jobs.'

'I'm needing him too,' said the Duke, still trying to suppress his excitement, and hurried away to continue the search.

After an hour, his excitement gave way to anxiety. He had almost forgotten the reason why he wanted to see Magnus; the main thing was to find him.

'Where on earth can he be? He seems to have vanished,' he said to old Cowan. 'I've looked everywhere. I've even been up the hill to see if he was with Mr Skinnymalink. He couldn't have swum across to Little Sula, could he?'

Old Cowan shook his head. 'Och no! The laddie'll likely just be hiding somewhere,' he said soothingly. But there was a worried look in his eye. Magnus, unlike the Ferret, was not one to play pranks. 'Hold on; I'll come and give you a hand to look for him.'

And now the search was on in real earnest. Gradually, as the news spread, everyone joined in. They hunted under haystacks, in byres, in hen-houses and empty sheds, covering every corner of the island without finding a trace of the missing boy. It was like a game of hide-and-seek, but no one enjoyed playing it.

Everyone took part: the minister, the District Nurse, the Ferret, the Hermit, the schoolmaster, even Mr Ebenezer Smith hobbling with his stick. Gran went about with her lips set tight and a worried frown on her brow, not saying a word.

It was Jinty, of course, who gave way to tears. For once she did not care a button what she looked like. Her face was smudged, her stockings torn, and her heart heavier than lead. 'I never even gave him his new gravat,' she sobbed, sitting down on the doorstep and burying her face in her hands. 'I'll never see him again, never!'

Andrew Murray, searching amongst the empty boats on the beach, suddenly felt someone tugging at his coat-tails. It was Tair. His face was white and he was trembling all over.

'What is it?' asked the schoolmaster, taking hold of the small boy's hand.

'Please, sir,' gulped Tair. 'Avizandum knows.'

'What does he know?' asked Andrew Murray gently. This was no time to scoff at Tair's imaginary companion. 'Tell me, Tair. Is it about Magnus?'

The boy gave a shiver. He appeared to be listening to Avizandum talking in his pocket. 'Blood! Oh dear! Round by the rocks. If we don't hurry, it'll be too late.'

Tair tugged at the teacher's hand and hurried him away, past the boats, past the place where Magnus and the old seal used to lie. They had to wade through pools, slipping and sliding over the sea-weed, scrambling over sharp rocks, with the teacher gritting his teeth as his lame leg began to sting with pain. But he scarcely felt it. The main thing was to find Magnus.

Suddenly they heard a strange barking sound. It came from Old Whiskers, swaying from side to side at the water's edge, grunting and wailing as if in anguish.

'Look! there's the blood,' cried Tair. 'In the water.'

Andrew Murray had already seen the splash of red and the inert body lying half-in half-out of the water. His heart almost stopped beating at the sight of it. Then he pulled himself up and turned to Tair. 'Go and fetch help,' he said urgently. 'Get the Duke and the others. Quick!' But was it already too late?

Tair sped off on his mission, and the schoolmaster hurried forward, not knowing whether he was going to find Magnus dead or alive. Old Whiskers gazed at him, gave a grunt of relief, and flopped back into the sea. He floated about near the shore, raising his head now and again so that he could watch what was happening.

There was no sign of life in Magnus. Andrew Murray bent over the boy's body and saw the blood was seeping from a deep wound in his forehead. His face was drained of all colour, and already he seemed to be away in another world. What had happened? Had he dived into the water and hit his head against a rock?

Andrew felt the boy's pulse. There was a faint flutter, so faint that it seemed as if Magnus's life was ebbing away. Even if help came quickly, his wound was too deep to be attended to on the island. A blood-transfusion would be needed; perhaps an operation. Somehow they would have to get him to hospital on the mainland.

The Duke and the others came running across the rocks. Gran pushed past them all and knelt down to cradle the body in her arms.

'My poor laddie! My poor wee laddie!' she repeated over and over again. But Magnus did not hear her.

They carried him carefully up to her cottage; and then it all began to happen. It was the Duke who took control. Ignoring his dislike of the telephone, he kept the lines of the post-office busy while he rapped out urgent orders to the mainland.

An air-ambulance? Yes! a helicopter could be sent at once. A bed in the Cronan Cottage Hospital? Yes! there would be one ready, with doctors and nurses standing by for an emergency operation.

Meanwhile, the District Nurse did what she could; but she shook her head sadly when she felt the feeble pulse. It would be a miracle if Magnus reached the hospital in time.

9 Jig-saw Puzzle

Magnus was – where? In some never-never land swimming with the seals.

He could taste the salt water in his mouth and feel Old Whiskers' body brushing against his as they tumbled together in the sea. He dived below the surface to tickle the young seals on their sleek stomachs. But was there one time when he dived too deep and did not come up?

Magnus seemed to be in a long dream different from any he had ever dreamt in his small bedroom in Gran's cottage. This was stranger and yet more real than any ordinary dream. Everything was sharper. Colours were brighter, voices were clearer, even his sense of smell seemed stronger.

Now he was no longer in the sea but floating gently in the air. Not alone. There were pictures all around him, and people. What a gentle voice his mother had, with a Highland lilt in it! Her hair was more golden than he had painted it in the picture. His father had a deep voice and a twinkle in his sea-blue eyes. His parents were both speaking to him, but what they were saying he could not understand. He tried to answer back, but he could not find his voice.

The pictures and the people faded, and then there was nothing.

The dreams came and went. Sometimes Magnus heard other voices nearer at hand. Gran saying: 'Wheesht, laddie, wheesht! Lie still!' The Duke seemed to be there, too, and someone with a deeper voice saying, 'Keep an eye on him, nurse. It's touch and go.'

Touch and go. It would have been easier to let go than to try to find his way back through the maze. He could just slip away with a sigh.

'Hang on, laddie; hang on.'

A work-roughened hand gripped his and held it tight. Was it Gran's? He had never heard her speak so gently before, with a sob in her voice.

'Yes, Gran, I'll try,' he wanted to tell her.

Years later – or so it seemed to Magnus – he opened his eyes. For a time he could not focus them on anything except a white ceiling. Sunbeams were playing on it, making patterns which shifted and changed like moving pictures.

He lay staring at them for a while; then he heard a whispering voice: 'Hullo, Magnus.'

Magnus tried to swivel his eyes to see where the voice came from. There was another bed near his, all neat and white, in which someone was tidily tucked up. The face on the pillow seemed faintly familiar and so did the whispering voice. 'Magnus, it's me.'

Who? It was not someone from Sula. Magnus lay and puzzled. Then suddenly he said in a weak voice that did not sound like his own: 'Wee Willy!' The boy from Cronan High School. 'What are you doing here?'

'I'm ill,' Wee Willy told him. 'So are you, Magnus.'

Ill! Magnus tried to think what had happened to him, but his head began to hurt, and once more he floated away into that strange limbo-land full of cottonwool clouds.

'Quiet, laddie; lie still!'

The next time he opened his eyes he heard himself moaning and saw Gran sitting bolt upright in a hard chair beside his bed. It was surprising to see her sitting still doing nothing and to hear her calling him laddie. What had happened to the work on the croft? Had she milked Tibby the cow and fed the calves, and brought in the peat? He would have to get up and help her.

'It's all right, laddie. I'll get the nurse. Lie still.'

Magnus lay still, wondering what it was all about. It was not the District Nurse who came in and bent over his bed. It was a young nurse with a round cheerful face. She was all dressed up like an angel, with a white halo round her head.

She smiled at him and said, 'Good for you, Magnus. You're coming round ...' But he was away again before he could answer her back.

For a long time Magnus seemed to come and go, not sure which were dreams and which reality. Had Gran really been there, holding his hand and speaking to him so gently? The Duke, too, had been by the bedside – or was that in a dream? – saying over and over again, 'Hold on, boy! Hold on.'

One day he woke up and felt a faint fragrance in the air. The scent of roses. There they were, a great bunch of them, arranged in a glass jug on a little table where he could look at them. They made a bright splash of colour in the clean clinical room. Deep scarlet, yellow and pink. Still life.

For a long time Magnus lay and looked at them, not even wondering where they came from. They gave him a satisfied feeling, as if he had been hungry and was now fed. Every petal was fashioned so perfectly. The shadings from pale to deeper pink were so delicately achieved that he could have admired them for ever.

A rustle from the other bed! Magnus turned his head.

'Willy, are you there?'

'Yes, Magnus; I'm here.'

Magnus tried to raise himself up but he seemed to have no power over his body. After a while he made another attempt to speak. 'Where are we, Willy?'

'In the hospital.'

'What hospital?'

'The Cottage Hospital at Cronan.'

Cronan!

A desolate feeling came over Magnus as he realized he was on the mainland far away from Sula. How had he got here and why was he lying still doing nothing? He must get up and go home. Gran would need him.

'I'll have to go back,' he said, struggling to raise his head.

'Oh no, Magnus, you can't,' said Wee Willy in a frightened voice. 'You've been very ill. You nearly died.'

Died! Magnus wanted to tell Wee Willy it was nonsense. He had never been ill in his life; but he was too weak to argue. He took a look at the boy in the other bed and asked, 'What are you doing here, Willy?'

'I'm ill, too. Pneumonia, I think it's called. But I'm better now. I can sit up.'

To prove it, Wee Willy struggled to raise himself into a sitting position. His hair was tousled and his face very pale as he leaned back against the pillows.

The cheerful nurse came bustling in. 'Well now, that's a good sign!' she said brightly. 'You're coming on, Willy.' She turned to the other bed. 'What about you, Magnus?'

'I'm fine.'

She smiled at him and felt his pulse. 'Yes, you're getting stronger. Keep still, Magnus, while I change your bandage.' He felt her gentle hands deftly swathing a soothing bandage round his throbbing head. Then she held a glass to his lips and made him swallow some liquid. 'Now you must have a little rest. You've got a visitor coming.'

It was Gran. Not in a dream but as real as could be. She was wearing her Sunday clothes. Her good blacks, she called them. When Magnus opened his eyes after his rest she was sitting, stiff as a poker, by his bed with a basket on her knees. How had she got here? She must have come across in the *Hebridean*.

'Hullo, Gran.' He turned his bandaged head to look at her.

'Hullo, laddie.' There was a break in her voice as if she was swallowing a lump in her throat. She put out her hand and Magnus clung to it like an anchor. He wanted to ask her a hundred questions, but his mind was still too confused. He just lay and looked at her.

Presently her face became blurred and he drifted off once more into a dream. When he came round again she was still there, laying the contents of her basket on the table beside the flowers. A pot of jam, a pat of butter, pancakes, scones, shortbread. He would not be able to eat them yet, but maybe Wee Willy would enjoy them.

Gran came back and sat down by his bedside, buttoning up her coat.

'Are you going away, Gran?'

'I'll come back, laddie,' she promised.

But he did not want her to leave him. 'Can I not come home with you, Gran?'

'Not for a wee while, laddie.'

The wee while stretched into endless days and weeks. For a long time Magnus seemed to have no control over his own body. He had to be fed and washed like a baby. When he tried to sit up his head hurt and the faint feeling came over him again. But gradually, as his mind cleared, he began to piece together all that had happened to him.

'I was swimming with the seals,' he said one day to Wee Willy who was sitting up in bed playing with a jigsaw puzzle.

'So you were, Magnus,' said Willy, smiling across to him.

'Did I hit my head on a rock?' puzzled Magnus.

'Yes, I think so. But you're looking a lot better now.'

'When will I get home?' It was the thought that was uppermost in Magnus's mind.

'Oh, I don't know,' said Wee Willy uneasily. To divert Magnus's attention he said, 'Look! you've got some more flowers.'

Sweet-peas this time, in shades of pink and blue and rosy-red.

'Where did they come from?' asked Magnus.

'There's a card with them. Wait! I'll get it for you. I'm allowed out of bed now.'

Wee Willy laid aside his jig-saw, scrambled out of bed and fetched the card. 'I'll read it for you, if you like, Magnus. It's from London and it says: GET WELL SOON. GREETINGS. EBENEZER SMITH.'

At first the name meant nothing to Magnus. Then he remembered. 'Him!' he said, averting his eyes from the flowers. He did not want to look at them again. The pain came back into his head and he looked so pale that Wee Willy said anxiously, 'Are you not feeling well, Magnus? Wait! I'll ring for the nurse.'

Every time he caught sight of the flowers, the worry about Ebenezer Smith and his Enterprises came back into Magnus's mind. Why was *he* sending flowers? Was it because he was still hoping to take over Sula?

It was a relief to Magnus when the sweet-peas withered to be replaced by an untidy bunch of mixed blooms brought by the old gardener from Cronan Castle, 'with the compliments of His Grace'.

There was no word from the little Duke himself; but every day other messages and parcels came. As Magnus grew stronger he was able to open them and read them himself without the aid of Wee Willy or the nurse.

The first time he laughed was when he read the Ferret's letter. It was only a few words scrawled on a smudged piece of paper torn from his school jotter. But it must have been a great effort for the untidy red-headed boy to write anything at all. Spelling was not the Ferret's strongest point.

'Dear Magnus Macduff, its a pitty your ill. I have nobdy to fihgt. The minster boxed my eers ystrday. I had brok his windo. Its quite here without you. Come home soon. Ill lend you my catpult. Yours faihtfull Ferret.'

Jinty wrote oftener in a flowery hand. 'Oh Magnus, I'm awful glad to hear you're feeling a bit better. I was wanting to come across in the *Hebridean* to see you but Gran would not let me. I'm being very good, helping her on the croft seeing you're not here.' Jinty could never resist giving herself a little pat on the back. 'The calves are quite big, and the twins are on their feet, but they can't walk far without falling down. Sheltie's okay. Tair's got a boil on his neck ...'

On and on. It was almost as if Jinty was talking in her non-stop way; but it was the kind of letter Magnus enjoyed reading in his hospital bed. Every small detail brought Sula nearer to him, but not near enough. Every day his longing for home grew stronger.

There was a postscript to Jinty's letter. 'I'm sending you something in a parcil. I made it myself. It got a bit dirty, but I've washed it.' There was a row of crosses for kisses at the end of the letter.

When the 'parcil' arrived it contained the knitted scarf, dropped stitches and all. 'Silly wee thing!' thought Magnus; yet he wore the scarf round his shoulders when he sat up in bed.

'My! you look a treat, Magnus,' said the nurse when she came in with a tray. 'You've got more colour in your cheeks.'

'When can I get home?' It was a question Magnus asked her and the doctor every day, a question to which he never got a direct answer.

'Oh, in a wee while. You're coming on. But you're still not out of the wood.'

As the days dragged by it seemed a very deep dark wood to Magnus. He had never in his life been so inactive for such a length of time. He lay puzzling his head about many things. It was like trying to piece together one of Wee Willy's jig-saw puzzles. How had he got from Sula to the Cottage Hospital? How serious was his illness? Where was the Duke? He had been here, surely, while Magnus lay in his strange dream, but now there was no sign of him.

Then one day the cheerful nurse brought in the mail. 'A postcard for you from London,' she told Magnus. 'Look! there's a picture of Buckingham Palace on it.'

Buckingham Palace looked even bigger than Cronan Castle and in a better state of repair. Magnus stared at it for some time, then his heart beat faster when he turned the card over and recognised the Duke's school-boy hand.

'Glad to hear you are improving. Had to go to London on business. Years and years since I've been here. Will tell you all about it soon. Hang on, boy. P.S. That fellow Smith sends his greetings. He's not such a bad chap, after all.'

A great depression descended on Magnus after reading the card over and over again. London! Business! That fellow Smith! It could only add up to one thing. The little Duke had given in. Sula would soon be taken over by Ebenezer Smith Enterprises.

It was such a setback that he sank into a period of listlessness during which he scarcely spoke, even to Wee Willy. The nurse tried her best to cheer him up and coax him to eat, but he turned his head away, and lay

back on his pillows, looking pale and drawn. He seemed
to have lost all interest in life.

'My! you're looking awful peaky,' said Mrs Reekie,
who called one day with a bunch of grapes. 'I was just
saying to Willy Reekie I'd better go and see for myself
how Magnus is getting on. I hear it was touch and go.
I must say you look like a ghost. Auntie Jessie and wee
Ailsa wanted to come, too, but Willy Reekie thought
they would maybe be too much for you.'

Willy Reekie was right! Even Mrs Reekie – well-
meaning though she was—was too much for Magnus.
As she burbled on and on, his head began to throb and
his hospital bed seemed to be floating in the air. Long
after she had gone he could still hear her talking.

'They say the Duke's away to London. Fancy! I
wonder what he's up to? Maybe he's visiting the royal
family. I hope he's dressed himself up a bit. I was just
saying to Willy Reekie ...'

The day came when Wee Willy was allowed to go
home. 'I'll leave you my jig-saws, Magnus; and I'll
come back and see you soon,' he said as he left. 'Hurry
up and get better.'

The jig-saws lay unheeded. There were enough
puzzles in Magnus's own mind. Left alone, he lay with
closed eyes trying to recall all the familiar sights of Sula.
But his vision of them was blurred. He could only see
gaudy shops and cafés, holiday-châlets, and noisy trippers. Even Gran's cottage was knocked down and replaced by a smart new hotel. Old Whiskers was nowhere
to be seen.

It was John Craigie, the Art Master from Cronan
High School, who jolted him out of his apathy. He
came one day, untidy as ever, carrying a carelessly

wrapped parcel under his arm. It contained a new drawing-book, and a set of pencils and paints.

'I thought you might like to do some scribbling while you've got a bit of time on your hands,' he said, concealing his alarm when he say how pale and wan the boy looked. He sat down by the bedside. 'I hear from Andrew Murray that you've done some splendid drawings for his book. It's going to be published, you know. Illustrated by Magnus Macduff. Isn't that great?'

Magnus showed a flicker of interest, more for the Sula schoolmaster's sake than his own. But, as the Art Master went on talking, he found it difficult to concentrate on what the man was saying.

'I was hoping you'd come back to the High School after the holidays, Magnus. But perhaps you'll need a month or two at home to regain your strength, and then we'll see.'

'Uh-huh!' said Magnus wearily. He could not think of the future.

John Craigie went away with an uneasy feeling at his heart. The best pupil he had ever had at the High School! Was he going to lose him forever?

Yet, he had brought Magnus the finest medicine in the world.

The boy lay and looked at the drawing-book; then he stretched out his hand towards it and propped himself up into a sitting position. The moment he opened the book and picked up a pencil some of his listlessness vanished.

At first he could only draw a feeble line or two. But soon there were crabs, crows, seals, seagulls, and wild geese streaking across the pages. Now and again a disturbing note crept in. When he tried to draw the beach, it seemed to be crowded with people under coloured umbrellas; but he scrubbed them out and turned his attention instead to the prehistoric creatures he had seen in the Glasgow museum, or to the flowers from Cronan Castle on his bedside table.

Now that he had found an occupation to absorb him he spent long hours sitting up with Jinty's scarf over his shoulders, filling page after page with drawings. He began to look less pale and peaky, though he was still very weak and at nights had restless dreams about Sula. Every day he waited for word from the Duke, hoping for another postcard but dreading the news it might contain.

He was stippling the markings on a butterfly's wings in his drawing-book one day when the nurse poked her head round the door and give him a bright smile.

'A special visitor for you, Magnus.'

The Duke came bounding in like a schoolboy, dressed in his shabbiest tweeds, with his deer-stalker hat stuck on the back of his head. He pulled the hat off, tossed it up to the ceiling and gave a whoop that could be heard all over the hospital.

'Hooray! I'm back! My goodness! am I glad to see you, Magnus! How are you, boy?'

He rushed to the bedside and clasped Magnus by the hand. In his delight at seeing him, Magnus forgot everything else. He scattered the drawings out of the way, held on to the little man's hand and said, 'Oh Duke, it's great to have you back.'

The Duke took a closer look at Magnus's pinched face and said anxiously, 'You're feeling better, aren't you, boy? I hated having to go to London just when you were so ill. But I waited till I was sure you were out of danger. You're all right, aren't you?'

'Uh-huh! I'm fine,' said Magnus, brushing the subject of his health aside. The moment had come when he must ask the dreaded question. 'Have you – did you sell it, Duke?'

'Yes, boy, yes!' said the Duke triumphantly. 'That's why I had to go to London to see that fellow. It's all signed and settled.'

Magnus gave him a stricken look and sank back, as white as one of the hospital sheets. His nightmare had become a reality. Sula – his own island paradise – was lost and gone for ever.

'What's the matter, boy?' asked the Duke in alarm.

'I thought,' said Magnus in a weak voice, 'I thought you didn't like him.'

'Who?' asked the Duke, looking puzzled.

'Ebenezer Smith.'

'Ebenezer Smith!' cried the Duke. 'Oh, he's not such a bad fellow. Bumped into him in London. In Piccadilly, of all places. He's improved, I can tell you that. Not half so bumptious. Must have been the air of Sula that did it. He was very worried about you. Kept asking how you were.' The little Duke jumped from one foot to the other and said, 'But why are we wasting time talking about him? I've got more important things to tell you.'

'What – what about?' asked Magnus, fearing what the answer might be.

'About that fellow Briggs. Sir Ronald Briggs, the music man. Wait till I show you.' He fumbled in the inner recesses of his old jacket and brought forth a crumpled roll of music. 'There! The Sula Symphony,' he said, laying it triumphantly on the bed. 'It's dedicated to you, Magnus. Look! there's your name. Sir Ronald has arranged for it to be played by a symphony orchestra – a royal command performance, no less. You'll have to get well enough to come with me. It's all due to you, boy.'

'Oh, Duke!' Magnus's mind was in a whirl of relief and happiness. It began to race like an over-heated motor. He could find no words to express his feelings beyond, 'Good for you, Duke. It's great!' And the greatest thing of all was that Sula was safe. Or was it? He had to make doubly sure. 'You'll never sell Sula?'

'Never, boy, never! Can't wait to get back there.' The little Duke beamed at him. 'Tell you what, boy, we'll go across together as soon as you're on your feet. It's the best cure in the world, a breath of Sula air.'

10 A Breath of Sula Air

'Magnus, will you be coming to the school today?'

Jinty Cowan poked her head round Gran's door and spoke to Magnus in a wheedling voice. Her hair was in ringlets, and she was wearing her best Fair Isle jumper and tartan skirt, with a string of blue beads round her neck and a dab of scent behind her ears. Irresistible!

'I'll see,' said Magnus cautiously.

He was at the kitchen table, supping his porridge from a bowl. Gran had set another bowl of creamy milk beside it so that he could dip his horn spoon, time and about, into the porridge and into the milk.

'Sup up every drop,' Gran had told him before she went out to feed the calves and the hens. 'It'll put some stuffing into you.'

By the look of him, Magnus was needing some stuffing. He seemed to have stretched out till he was all skin and bones. But already, since he had returned to the island, there was a sparkle in his eyes and more colour in his cheeks. Gran's feeding and the good air of Sula would soon work wonders.

'Try and come,' said Jinty, giving him an enticing smile. 'I'll expect you.' Seeing there was no response, she was about to take herself off. Then she turned and said, 'It's great to have you back, Magnus.' This time there was no coquettishness in her voice. She meant it from the heart.

Magnus gave her an embarrassed glance and swallowed a mouthful of porridge. He recognized her genuine feeling but did not know how to acknowledge it. It was a relief when she went away and left him alone in the kitchen.

He looked up at the picture on the wall. The peat fire was burning brightly, throwing flickers of light on the images of his parents. He seemed to know them better now, though he could see the faults in the picture. His mother's hair should have been brighter and his father's eyes bluer, but the likeness was there. They appeared to be watching him, almost as if they were about to say – as Gran had done – 'Sup up every drop.'

Presently Gran came stumping into the kitchen in her big boots, carrying a pail in each hand. She looked at him sharply and said, 'Did you finish your porridge?'

'Yes, Gran,' he said meekly.

There were no more soft words from her now that the boy was out of danger. Things had reverted to normal, and somehow Magnus was glad that he and Gran were back on their old terms. It was nice to know that she was fond of him and could call him laddie on special occasions, but it was not for every day.

Soon she would be ordering him about. 'Mag-nus, go and collect the eggs. Magnus, have you mended the fence? Mag-nus, dig up the potatoes.' But not yet; he was still too shaky on his feet.

'Where are you going?' she asked, as he got up from the table and made for the door.

'Nowhere. Just out.'

'You'd better not catch cold.' She picked up Jinty's scarf which was hanging over the winter-dyke. 'Here! take the gravat.'

'Oh Gran, I don't want it.'

'You'll take it,' she said firmly and flung it round his neck. As she tucked it around him, her touch became more gentle. Their eyes met, and Magnus gave her a flicker of a smile.

'Thanks, Gran,' he said, and went out into the clear morning air.

It was good to feel the freshness on his face and the salt tang in the breeze. Every breath he took seemed to give him strength, and each familiar sight satisfied his eye. The great expanse of sky, the ducks dibbling in the water, the bright-red rowans in the Manse garden, the burnt-brown bracken on the Heathery Hill, the young calves frisking in Gran's field.

Rory, the collie, was keeping guard like a nursemaid on the McCallum twins who were tottering about on unsteady legs outside their door. Old Cowan, splitting sticks with a great axe, looked up at the boy as he passed, and said, 'Ay, Magnus, it's great to see you on your feet again. You're looking more like yourself already.'

Magnus nodded to him and went on down to the beach. He did not need to whistle for Old Whiskers. The seal was there already waiting for him, slithering on to the rock and swaying from side to side in his delight at seeing the boy.

'It's all right, Whiskers. I'm here.'

The two of them snuggled down in perfect harmony. All the troubled nightmares of the past were gone.

The school-bell began to ring. The seal raised his head at the sound of it, and so did the boy. The bell seemed to be calling, 'Magnus! Magnus! Come! Come!'

Magnus hesitated. Should he go back and sit at his old desk? Nothing had been said or could be settled about his future. There could be no talk about going back to the High School at Cronan till he was stronger. Meanwhile, his old place in the little schoolroom was waiting for him.

So was Jinty Cowan.

'Please, sir, Magnus may be coming,' she whispered to the teacher on the way in. 'Oh, I hope he does. Don't you not, Mr Murray?' She had given up all thought, for the time being, of transferring herself to the Girls' High School. As long as Magnus was in Sula, she would stick close by him.

Andrew Murray looked up at her and said firmly, 'Go to your place, Jinty.' He was hoping as much as Jinty that Magnus might come, but he was not going to force the issue nor was he going to let Little Miss Know-All see how important it was.

He opened the register, then took out the tawse. When

the class saw the dreaded Hangman's Whip lying on his desk as an awful warning, they settled down and sat with folded arms, looking as if butter would not melt in their mouths, waiting for their names to be called out.

The Ferret could not sit still for long. Below the desk he kicked out at Tair sitting in front of him, but the young boy could not retaliate with the teacher's eye on him.

'You can sort him later,' whispered Avizandum from Tair's pocket. 'I've got a safety-pin in here!'

Jinty smoothed her ringlets and looked sentimentally at the empty desk in front of her, with the initials MM carved on it with a penknife. Magnus's old books lay there, with every margin covered with drawings of birds and beasts. She hunted in her pocket, then leant over and laid a liquorice-allsort beside his jotter. It was a kind of welcome-back present.

Suddenly she stretched up her neck like a swan till she could see out of the window.

'Please sir, he's coming!' she hissed to the teacher, and went pink with pleasure.

Magnus came slowly up the road towards the little school, still not sure if his feet would take him inside or whether he would walk past. The District Nurse scooshed towards him on her bicycle and called out, 'It's great to see you up and about, Magnus. Don't catch cold. You're wise to wear that scarf.'

When she had cycled past, Magnus unwound the scarf. He was not going into the classroom wearing *that* round his neck. The Ferret would snigger at him. He looked over the dyke and caught sight of Flora Macdonald standing in old Cowan's field. On an impulse, he climbed over and went towards her.

'There!' he said, winding the scarf round her neck. 'It can keep *you* warm. I'm not needing it any more.'

A gaunt figure waved to him as he went past the schoolhouse garden. Mr Skinnymalink. He and the little Duke were sitting together on an old wooden bench, enjoying the morning sunshine without needing to speak to each other.

'Okay, boy?' the Duke called out.

'Yes, Duke. Okay!'

In the schoolroom Andrew Murray was calling out the register to the pupils who answered him in their different ways, the Ferret in a put-on squeaky voice. 'I'm here, sir.'

'Janet Cowan.'

'Present, sir,' said Jinty promptly, putting up her hand.

'Angus Alastair McCallum.'

'That's me,' said Tair, surprised as always to hear his correct name.

The door opened and Magnus came in. There was a little gasp of joy from Jinty, and a gleam in the Ferret's eyes as the boy walked past him to his accustomed place.

'Magnus Macduff,' said the teacher, trying to keep the same tone in his voice.

'Present,' said Magnus, and opened his jotter. When he saw the kittiwakes and puffins flying in and out of his sums, he settled down with a little sigh of satisfaction. Then he picked up the liquorice-allsort and stuffed it down the back of the Ferret's neck.

He felt great.

Also by Lavinia Derwent
Sula 45p

This is the first book about Magnus and the island of Sula. Lessons
seem silly to the boy whose only interest is being outside
sketching the animals and sea-birds. But Magnus finds that the
people on the island — the sickly new teacher, the old hermit
Skinnymalink and Jinty — are just as important to him as the
animals ...

Return to Sula 25p

In this next book about Magnus, he finds out more about his dead
parents whom he has never seen. He wins a competition with one
of his pictures and is persuaded to visit the mainland where he
meets the Duke, who has a photograph of his mother and father.
Gran never talks about them — in fact she hardly ever talks at all —
but she comes out of her shell when she sees a painting of
Magnus's one night while he is out in the storm rescuing his worst
enemy.

You can buy these and other Piccolo books from booksellers and
newsagents ; or direct from the following address :
Pan Books, Cavaye Place, London SW10 9PG
Send purchase price plus 15p for the first book and 5p for
each additional book, to allow for postage and packing
Prices quoted are applicable in UK